RETURN OF A GANGSTER'S GIRL

RETURN OF A GANGSTER'S GIRL

Chunichi

www.urbanbooks.net

Urban Books
1199 Straight Path
West Babylon, NY 11704

ISBN-13: 978-1-60162-027-9
ISBN-10: 1-60162-027-6

First Printing December 2007
Printed in the United States of America

10 9 8 7 6

Submit Wholesale Orders to:
Kensington Publishing Corp.
C/O Penguin Group (USA) Inc.
Attention: Order Processing
405 Murray Hill Parkway
East Rutherford, NJ 07073-2316
Phone: 1-800-526-0275
Fax: 1-800-227-9604

Dedication

This book is dedicated to the victims and love ones of those affected by the Virginia Tech tragedy.

Acknowledgments

By now you all should know the routine; so here we go. First I would like to thank God for blessing me with such a wonderful talent and allowing me to reach so many. The roller coaster I was once on has become a smooth ride and without Him none of this would have been possible.

Thank you to my fans. Without you all there is no me. I appreciate all of the continuous support.

Shout outs to my literary family, Carl Weber, Roy Glenn, the super agent, Marc Gerald, and my big sis, Nikki Turner. A special thanks to Joylynn Jossel for all of her editing expertise.

Thanks to my extended family and friends. All my girls back in the A, and the Nanston Naughty girls, even though I'm gone you guys are still showing support. Now that is real! NeNe and the Major Creations crew, thanks for keeping the head tight and books in rotation. You know it's that beauty salon gossip that really gets the word out! To my friends for life, Kicia, Tracey, Chele, Melanie, Sara, Toya, Meisha thanks for being not only friends but sisters. To my brother by another mother, Dante' Davis, thanks for being there no matter how bad I treat you. You

ACKNOWLEDGMENTS

know it's just the *girl* in me. Can't forget Stephanie, Tasha, and Sophie; you girls are definitely one of a kind. To all my Jamaican massive, back home and in the U.S., big up!

To my family, I give never ending thanks. I love you guys! Mom you're always by my side standing proud and telling everyone you know about the books. You still show the same excitement now as you showed the very first book. Don't worry there will soon be a book you can tell your "church folk" to buy ☺. Dad, thanks for making me the firecracker I am. To my baby bro, Vincent, forget those tacky ho's; your sister's the Urban Diva! To my loving husband, Aron, I know I pluck the hell out of your nerves, yet you're always so patient and understanding. It takes a special man to deal with such a spoiled chick. A girl couldn't ask for anything more.

Ain't nothing changed, so finally the middle finger to the haters!

Prologue

Run, run as fast as you can. You can't catch me, I'm the Gingerbread Man, Ceazia recited as she hit the streets of Virginia and heard the constant rumors of people out to get her. She had to wonder if people had really forgotten her legacy and truly didn't recognize who she was. Maybe they needed to check her résumé. She'd earned and worn the title as a Gangster's Girl way too long for people not to know. Then after losing her gangster she still stood her ground because she realized she was now married to the game. Then when she came down to the wire she didn't crack, she wasn't ashamed, she told shit how it was. Her life was nothing but the truth, the naked truth. There wasn't a time she didn't come out on top. She knew what she wanted and always got it. So what if it was at the expense of a few miserable lives. With the entire state against her, Ceazia was still invincible. She was back in VA with a vengeance. It was the return of a gangster's girl. So to Danielle, Snake, Judah or any other that wanted to test her, she welcomed the challenge because she knew she was faster than the fucking Gingerbread Man. But what she didn't remember about the story is in the end the Gingerbread Man was outsmarted by the sly fox!

Chapter 1

"Let me get two bottles of Rosé. That's one bottle for each of those haters over there mean muggin.' " Ceazia laughed while pointing at two chicks that stood staring at her from the bar as she placed her order with the chubby waitress that served the VIP section of the club. "Let 'em hate on me even more as I sip on these two bottles while between the two of them, they can't even afford one."

"Excuse me?" the waitress responded to Ceazia's request with plenty of attitude as though Ceazia's comment had been directed towards her instead of the two broads at the bar.

"Two . . ." Ceazia held up two fingers, "bot-tles of Ro-sé." She spoke to the waitress as though she was retarded or hard of hearing, using her fingers to make up sign language.

"They are one-fifty each; One . . . five . . . zero each," the waitress replied, lips twisted and head tilted to the side as she held up each number with her hand as if she was now doing sign language. She then continued. "Are you sure you want two?" the waitress spat, looking Ceazia up and down—insinuating that Ceazia couldn't possibly afford the two bottles of Rosé she'd ordered.

"Looks like we have another hater," Diamond, who was sitting right next to Ceazia, whispered in Ceazia's ear after taking note of the comment the waitress had just made.

"Damn, you know what? You're right?" Ceazia said, scratching her head as if rethinking her request. "I may need to order three bottles. It looks like we have an additional hater who has just joined the crowd. But I don't know if I can blame her. I mean, look at her." Ceazia gave the waitress the once-over. "If I was fat and ugly, I would hate a bitch like me too." Ceazia laughed, and without saying another word or even looking in the waitress's direction, she held up two fingers in her face, confirming the fact that she still wanted two bottles of Rosé champagne.

Ceazia didn't even bother to further entertain the obvious ignorance of the waitress as she just stood there glaring at Ceazia as if she was going to react to the way Ceazia had just dissed her.

Hell, maybe a bitch really should order three bottles, Ceazia thought with a snicker. *Two for the haters and an additional one to crack across the head of this bitch's hatin' ass.* It wasn't clear if the waitress had come to her senses and decided to just keep it rolling or if she'd gotten the picture that Ceazia's word was final, but after Ceazia moved the two fingers so close to the waitress's nose that she almost touched it, the chick said no more and eventually just stomped away, rolling her eyes and sucking her teeth.

Diamond and Ceazia sat at Club Reign and watched as the crowd grew thicker as the night got later. They kept their eyes glued to the door. It was just about twelve o'clock and the club had almost reached its capacity. They knew in a few more minutes the doors would be shut and the only ones that would get in at that point were the true ballers that were able to break enough bread to change security's mind about opening the doors. And that was the moment they were waiting for. Like a fiend desperate for a hit, Ceazia and Diamond would be on the ballers; getting first dibs. It was nothing for the two of them to tag-team a nigga just to get in his pockets. Diamond and Ceazia had only been comrades a little more than a year, but it seemed like they'd known each other forever. They always knew what the other was thinking and they always shared the same point of view. And if there ever was a time when Diamond thought she felt differently about something than how Ceazia felt, it didn't take much for Ceazia to change Diamond's thought process.

Now that the unsuspected hater, little miss waitress, was gone, it was time for Ceazia to focus her attention back to the bar where the official haters, India and Carmen, two chicks that she used to roll tight with back in the day, sat. The looks on their faces were priceless once they had spotted Ceazia Devereaux in the flesh and blood; live and direct, right before their eyes. It was as though they had seen a ghost. They looked like a deer caught in the headlights of Ceazia's Hummer H2; frightened to death with no chance of survival.

"What the hell did you do to them?", Diamond asked Ceazia, noticing the looks on India and Carmen's faces.

"To be honest, I've never done anything directly to either of them," Ceazia stated, giving Diamond an indirect answer in hopes of avoiding telling her the real story behind the beef; they suspected her of killing Meikell, once a friend to them all. "I think they're just surprised to see me. I don't know if it's from the embarrassment of how I'm high rollin' compared to them, or just my mere presence alone that's got them shook." Ceazia took a sip of her white Zinfandel she had been babysitting as she examined the two women one by one and then she continued with her reasoning. "Those chicks used to be my homegirls, and from the looks of things, much hasn't changed since a few years ago when we used to hang. I wouldn't be surprised if those bitches were still driving the same car, living in the same old crib, working the same dead-end jobs and sucking the same dick. And when I say sucking the same dick, I mean the both of them sucking the same single dick!" Ceazia and Diamond both burst out in laughter.

"Wait!" Diamond said, after almost choking on her white Zinfandel. "What are we laughing at? We've sucked the same dick before."

Ceazia and Diamond continued to laugh, clinking their glasses together.

"Now don't get me wrong, I ain't knocking them for being stable, but if you and I are sucking the same dick, or any dick for that matter, there had better be some benefits." Ceazia pointed to India and Carmen. "And it is evident from their appearance that nothing is jumping. They are wearing the same old jewels and same old clothes. And the worse shit of all is that bag Carmen is carrying is a Gucci bag that *I* bought her. And to shovel more shit on top of a manure pile, I bought the bag damn nearly three years ago. Hell, I wouldn't be surprised if that is Iceberg she has on. Now you tell me why they look so corny. They done spent the last of their last getting up in VIP that they can't even buy a drink, so they standing around with dry mouths waiting on some nigga to offer to buy them a drink. But any real baller can see through their nostalgic-looking asses. Those hoes might as well have Jheri curls and shit."

Diamond wasn't as blunt and obvious as Ceazia, so she tried to discreetly observe the girls. After doing so, she shrugged her shoulders as if to say she had no defense for the chicks. They appeared to fit Ceazia's critique like a glove.

"Exactly," Ceazia continued. "Outdated tramps." She took another sip of her drink and then said, "I know they want to turn into an ostrich and just bury their little weave-filled heads!" Diamond and Ceazia laughed and threw back the last of their drinks. Five minutes hadn't passed before Ceazia caught yet another set of females staring in her direction.

"Damn!" Ceazia snapped. "Bitches are wearing the hate on thick tonight," she said to Diamond, noticing even another set of bitches whispering and pointing in her direction. "Is it because we're fly to death?"

"Maybe it's because you look like you just stepped off a rap video. I think they want your autograph," Diamond said, referencing Ceazia's latest look.

"Let's really give them something to talk about." Ceazia

looked over at Diamond with a mischievous smirk on her lips. Diamond ran her tongue inside her jaw and returned the smirk with a nod of her head.

Ceazia sensually slid her arm around Diamond's neck, not caring what the next person thought of their public display of female-to-female affection. If her luck was any good, she'd hope to catch the eye of some horny baller and turn him on. Diamond loved when Ceazia openly showed her feelings for her so she didn't mind playing right into things. She grabbed Ceazia around the waist and pulled her close as they tongued each other down. It was as though the DJ had cut off the record and the music had stopped. The entire club was focused on Ceazia and Diamond. After their intimate kiss, they both laughed as all the men looked like they wanted to pull out their hard dicks and jerk them while all the females twisted their lips and rolled their eyes in disgust.

Every since Ceazia had moved back to Virginia from Atlanta, she'd made it a habit of shining on a bitch every chance she got. Her long black hair had been replaced with a stylish mohawk and her basic conservative designer jeans and nice shirt style had been replaced with outlandish designer clothing like True Religion, BAPE, Red Monkey, and Ed Hardy, topped off with colorful accessories and a wild attitude. But one thing for sure had not changed; Ceazia's brick-house frame was still intact. Her small waistline hadn't grown an inch, her ass was just as thick and her breasts were just enough to give any man a mouthful. Ceazia always said it was hard being that bitch that everyone seemed to love to hate, but she didn't mind putting in the work it took to be that bitch.

As if the city hadn't hated the shit out of her before,

Ceazia had managed to gain a few silent enemies after Vegas's death and even more after Snake, Duke, and Bear's deaths. Yes, she was the one responsible for the deaths of four of the most popular men in Norfolk; men that niggas claimed to be the hardest cats in the city couldn't even take out, which made her the baddest bitch.

Vegas was her ex-boyfriend who she had loved more than her own life, which wasn't an easy deed for Ceazia, considering how much she loved herself. It was Vegas that had introduced her to the life of the streets. But when he fucked up and crossed the line and made a move on Meikell, Ceazia's best friend at the time, she lost it and put them both to rest. Then a year later Ceazia noticed that no man, not even Vegas's prior supplier, Bear, could ever compare to the lifestyle Vegas had provided for her, but she figured Vegas's brother, Snake, would come the closest. So with nothing but money on her mind, she set her sights after him. Knowing she would have to proceed with caution, Ceazia moved slowly to sink her claws into Snake, using his naive nephew, Duke, as a crutch while doing so. When it was all said and done, Ceazia had gotten herself in the middle of a murderous love triangle. But it just so happened that in this battle, like all the rest, she was the only one left standing.

It was apparent that people weren't feeling Ceazia. As a result of all the drama on the streets, the beef some had with Ceazia was considered silent. Not one of them had the balls to actually confront her with their speculations that she was behind the madness. It didn't take Ceazia long to hear the rumors on the streets, though. Ceazia had gotten branded and was known as a money-hungry psychotic bitch; a bitch that would rob a nigga and then, blind or in plain view, straight kill his ass. Now that was a hell of a title. Although Ceazia knew she'd done some grimy things in her day, she was still shocked to know that was what people were thinking of her. Surely other niggas on the streets had done worse. Who was she to become a hood legend?

As one could expect, a title like that left most females afraid to even look at her in the wrong way, and most niggas wanted no dealings. With the day-to-day bullshit they had to deal with from envious niggas on the streets there was no room for a vicious chick like Ceazia. The bitches didn't matter to Ceazia. She could handle them. But she needed every baller nigga she could get her hands on for money, so their opinion did, to some degree, matter.

After Ceazia's initiation to the game as a Gangster's Girl, hustling was the only way she knew for survival. She tried her hand at being the perfect girlfriend instead of a gold digger. She had even decided to follow the advice of those stupid-ass Destiny's Child bitches and cater to her man instead of running game, fucking and bucking, or any other quick-trick ideas she could pull out of her hat. But in the end, she got fucked—raw dog, up the ass, without even some warm spit as a lubricant. And anyone who knew Ceazia Devereaux knew that she was not one to get mad at the game or its players; she got even! You may have gotten one over on her, but you wouldn't live to talk about it.

After her ex-boyfriend, a former rapper named Parlay, broke her heart, Ceazia swore on everything she loved and owned that no nigga would ever get the chance to get over on her again. From that point on a guy could only provide her with money, and maybe a little dick. And that's only if she got tired of the strap-on that Diamond had recently introduced her to.

With so many haters and so many parties, it had become quite expensive for Ceazia to floss each night in hopes of catching the eye of her next victim. With her road dawg, Diamond, by her side, Ceazia made it a point to make a statement wherever they went and it was costing her at least three grand a party. Three grand is cool; ain't nothin' but a drop in the bucket when you have consistent money coming in, but it's a bitch when it only seems to be constantly going out. So as Ceazia partied, she scanned the club. And before she knew it, it was time for her next casualty in this game she had managed to get caught up in, but had a hell of a time getting out of.

Since she'd been to the A, she learned a few tricks and couldn't wait to test them out on just the right guy in VA.

"Two bottles of Rosé champagne?" the waitress said as she finally returned with Ceazia's order, placing the ice-filled bucket and two bottles on the table. She then placed two champagne glasses and a few napkins down with them. "Three hundred. Cash only." She held out her hand and rolled her neck. For some reason she thought that she was making it hard for Ceazia to pay for the champagne by demanding cash only.

Ceazia grinned and then dug into her oversized Chanel bag and pulled out one thousand dollars, all twenties. Then she quickly counted off fifteen twenties and placed them in the palm of the waitress's waiting hand. While the waitress counted the three hundred, Ceazia pulled off three more twenties and folded them. Once the waitress had confirmed all three hundred was there, Ceazia handed her the sixty dollars.

"Thank you." The waitress smiled after counting out the additional money, excited she'd received such a nice tip. "Let me know if you need anything else." She walked away, tucking the money down into her tip pocket.

"See how phony chicks are?" Diamond stated, noticing the waitress's sudden change of attitude.

"I know," Ceazia agreed. "But money talks, though, baby. Money talks." Ceazia filled each of their glasses and they drank up. She winked at the clique of haters. *Yeah, bitches, y'all stay thirsty sipping on those cheap-ass Coronas and shit while we floss on that ass.* Ceazia poured her and Diamond another glass and they toasted before drinking up again. "To us," Ceazia said, "bitches gettin' money."

"I'll drink to that!" Diamond agreed.

The party had just begun, and as it continued on, Ceazia spotted a familiar face enter through the club's doors. Although Ceazia was certain she had seen him before, she just couldn't place him. *Perhaps he only looks like somebody I know,* Ceazia thought as she eyed him down.

She watched the young man from the time he paid security to let him and his entourage in, until the time they all sat down in the VIP a few sections over from where Ceazia and Diamond were sitting. He didn't draw very much attention to himself, but he seemed quite mysterious. That alone intrigued Ceazia. A veteran to the game, she knew those were the ones to look out for. Niggas with the most to lose drew the least attention to themselves. They allowed their appearance and swagger to do all the talking for them.

The dude sat quietly smoking purple haze. The cloud of smoke lingered around his head like an angel's halo, but an angel he was anything but. Ceazia was getting a contact from just the scent of the smoke alone.

"Whew!" Diamond, the weed head, said, confirming that the weed he was smoking was nothing but the truth.

Surrounded by bottles of Cristal that the waitress wasted no time in supplying him, his boys continuously looked to him for drinks. They each stood around with at least two groupies each. But not Mr. Mysterious, cool, calm, and collected; he sat alone. Ceazia checked out each of his boys briefly to see if she recognized any of them. Not one did she recognize.

As the night went on, Ceazia and Diamond continued to party while constantly monitoring the guy in the corner. Ceazia knew she had to wait patiently for the perfect opportunity to approach him. The opportunity came when each of his boys were completely preoccupied with their groupies, either on the dance floor or getting head in the back of the club. At last, the young man was all alone and Ceazia could finally get to him with no interruptions.

"How do I look? Do I need lip gloss? Is my face oily?" Ceazia asked Diamond while shuffling though her purse for her M•A•C makeup bag.

"Baby, you look fine," Diamond assured her. "Now go ahead and get your man. I've been watching you check him out all night. He's all yours, baby." Diamond smacked Ceazia on the ass and shoved her off.

Other chicks might have been jealous at the fact that their lover was about to go hook up with someone else, right in their face no less, but Diamond knew that Ceazia about to push up on ol' dude was all in the name of money. If Ceazia made a come up, then Diamond made a come up. And if it meant workin' a nigga, so be it!

Ceazia took her time walking toward the young man, all the while racking her brain trying to figure out where she knew him from. She never forgot a face, or at least she was never unable to place a face, which was a major skill in the business she was in. A girl didn't want to accidentally try to work the same nigga twice; although if any broad could pull that type of shit off, it would be Ceazia. Wherever she might have known the gentleman from, she only hoped it wasn't from any bad predicament.

With a few steps left to go before she was face to face with him, she took a deep breath and quickly rehearsed in her head what she would say. But before she could reach her Prince Charming, someone crossed her path and landed right into his lap. The woman that now sat cozy in dude's lap had a familiar face as well, but Ceazia had no doubt where she knew this bitch from. *What the hell was in that champagne? Or am I losing my touch?* Ceazia thought.

Embarrassed and unsure what to do, Ceazia stood motionless and watched as the woman, who she recognized as Danielle, the girlfriend of Snake at the time of his death, hugged all up on her dream guy. She didn't know what to do. The longer she stared at the girl, the more flashbacks of the night of Snake, Duke, and Bear's deaths rushed through Ceazia's head. The memory was as clear as yesterday as she looked at Danielle. The memory of her fleeing from the hotel and driving past Danielle on the way out surfaced her brain. The one second they met eye to eye seemed to last an hour. Ceazia wondered if Danielle would recognize her from that night.

As she continued to stare, Ceazia almost second-guessed herself. *Is that her?* Danielle had appeared to have gained a few pounds, but yeah, it definitely looked like her. And even Ceazia had to admit that she was wearing the extra weight well. Realizing the man she had set her eyes on all night had been snatched up from right underneath her nose, Ceazia decided to run back to her safe nest. Just as she was about to turn around, though, it hit her; she did know the guy from somewhere. The man before her was named Shawn, a drug connect that, the last she knew of, supplied most of Norfolk. And he had it all; cocaine, weed, heroin, and even ecstasy. This nigga was definitely a pot of gold at the end of the rainbow.

Right as Ceazia was about to make her quick turn-around, Shawn looked up and locked eyes with her as he hugged Danielle. His look alone said it all. She read the words, *I want your sexy ass* in his eyes.

Ceazia returned the favor by giving him the most seductive look she could. Her eyes responded, "This sexy-body girl comes with a price." Then she walked away, ass bouncing each step of the way to give him a glimpse of what she had to offer.

"With that performance, how could he not want you?" Diamond said as Ceazia returned. "Fuck that bitch over there trying to ride his dick dry."

"I can't believe this shit," Ceazia spat between gritted teeth. "Somehow that bitch always manages to find her way down my path." Ceazia swallowed a glass of champagne.

"You know her?" Diamond inquired.

"Yeah, she was a little competition of mine with this certain fella, Snake, back in the day," Ceazia said, giving the least amount of information possible.

"What, someone was actually able to give you a run for your money?" Diamond said, full of disbelief.

"Sure, she slowed things down a little when it came to Snake, but this time I'll be sure give her a little taste of what it feels like to bitten by a snake like me."

"Okayyyyyyyy!" Diamond poured Ceazia another glass and they toasted.

They continued to party and Ceazia kept her eye on Shawn the entire time. She was not giving up. In fact, she wanted him even more now that she knew there was competition.

After an hour or so, Danielle finally walked away, giving Ceazia another opportunity at her prey. Ceazia and Diamond both stared as Danielle left her man helpless from the likes of the queen bee.

"From the looks of things, C, your little friend isn't going to be up for the battle," Diamond said, pointing at Danielle's swollen belly.

"Damn! How did I miss that? I must have really been focusing on Shawn not to have noticed that she is pregnant."

"Very pregnant! But I have to admit, she wears it well. From behind you would have never known. Guess that's how you missed it, huh?" Diamond giggled as Ceazia rolled her eyes.

Obviously jealous at how well Danielle looked even though she looked at least five months pregnant, Ceazia focused her attention back on Shawn now that he was game once again. Since Shawn had given her the eye, she knew roping him in would be a piece of cake. Ceazia took her time finishing her drink before she walked over. She didn't want to seem too desperate. As she took her last sip, she scanned over the crowd to see where Danielle was.

She didn't want to take the chance of her popping up again. Danielle was nowhere in sight, which meant she was either in the bathroom or gone. Ceazia hoped it was the latter. Either way it went, time was of the essence before another distraction prevented her from hitting her mark.

She stood up and straightened her clothes as she prepared to walk over to Shawn. When she looked up she was caught by another surprise. *Judah!* "What the fuck?" Ceazia said aloud, baffled by the strain of bad luck she was having in her attempt to hook, line, and sinker this one big fish.

She watched as Judah sat down beside Shawn and they proceeded to chat away.

"Dis is your last chance, you know. If dis don't go right, you must deal wit da big man," Judah said sternly.

"Cool, cool." Shawn nodded, assuring Judah that everything was good.

The conversation seemed kind of serious as Ceazia watched them closely. Judah appeared to be pissed, yet Shawn remained calm. After they finished talking, Judah walked off. Shawn pulled his cell phone out, said a couple words into the receiver, then the next thing Ceazia knew, him and his boys all headed towards the club exit from different directions of the club. Shawn didn't even look Ceazia's way as he walked right past her and out the VIP section. Ceazia watched as he exited through the club's side door.

"I wonder what that was all about," Diamond asked Ceazia as she walked up next to her, just as baffled by the scenario as Ceazia.

"I don't know," Ceazia replied, "but I'm tempted to follow them out the club and find out. Maybe if I can't get Shawn, I can grab Judah, with his fine ass!" Ceazia winked at Diamond.

"Let's do it," Diamond encouraged her.

With a look of agreement, Ceazia, along with Diamond, drank the last of their champagne and headed out the door right behind Shawn and his crew.

Judah was the first in Ceazia's sight as they exited the club. She couldn't help but reflect on how fine he was. He was just as fine as the last day she'd seen him. She thought back to the days at the Mango Tree, a local reggae club where Judah played music back in the day.

"Judah is still fine as ever." She shared her thoughts with Diamond. "But when I left town, he was fucking with this lil' young chick name BJ. He loved her lil' ass to death. It must have been her innocence or something, because he was even throwing me shade when I was trying to give up the pussy."

"Damn, it was that serious, huh? He was passing up on your pussy?" Diamond said in disbelief. After all, she knew firsthand just how good Ceazia's pussy was.

"Tell me about it. The sad thing is that I kind of liked his lil' girlfriend. She was real cool. I looked at her like a lil' sister. I had no idea she was going to end up stepping on my toes," Ceazia said, making it seem as though BJ stole Judah from her.

"So you saying ol' girl knew you were diggin' on Judah before she got with him?"

"Not really. I mean, me and her met before she and Judah hooked up. I actually introduced them one night at the club. I had no idea they were going to hook up, though. She had a little boyfriend and everything. I guess

18

I should have spoken my piece so that she would have known what was up."

"Look, girl." Diamond interrupted Ceazia as she pointed toward the all-black Dodge Magnum sitting on black twenty-two-inch Giovannis with a deep gold lip that sat across the street from them as they stood posted up on the wall outside the club.

Ceazia looked up to see Judah leaning against the car, staring at her as he spoke on his cell phone. Ceazia decided to head his way. He didn't even blink as she walked toward him, crossing the street. By the time Ceazia was up on him, he had wrapped up his phone conversation.

"Judah!" she said to him. "Whagwon?" She asked him what was up, mimicking his native patois language.

"Wham, C?" he responded in an annoyed tone that said "What the fuck you want, Ceazia?"

"Nothing much. I was just wondering what was up with my girl, BJ. How is she?" Ceazia had every intention on hollering at Judah, but now she figured she'd better take things in a different direction since Judah didn't seem to be in the best of moods.

"Everting good, mon."

"That's good. Well, give her my number."

Judah rolled his eyes and then said, "Gimme it?" Although he was annoyed by Ceazia's presence, he was pleased to have her number to fall back on in case Shawn didn't hold up his end of the bargain. Shawn claimed he had some great moneymaking plan that involved Ceazia, but knowing her past, Judah knew he had to have a backup plan.

Ceazia read off her Atlanta area code cell phone number that hadn't yet been changed to a local Virginia number. She watched carefully as Judah placed his business phone, the first cell he had just been talking on, in a case on his waist and then entered her number into a black RAZR phone that he pulled out. Although she'd clearly stated that the number was for BJ, the number was stored exactly where she'd hoped it to be, in *his* phone. If things went how she'd planned, Judah would be the one calling her up and not BJ.

"Umph-umph," Diamond cleared her throat as she approached them after watching Judah save the number and close his phone.

"I'm sorry. Where's my manners? Judah, this is my girlfriend, Diamond," Ceazia introduced. Both she and Diamond looked at Judah seductively.

"Girlfriend aye? You fa get bullet fa dat in Jamaica?" Judah understood exactly what their eyes were saying and expressed the taboo of same-sex relationships in his native country of Jamaica.

"Well, welcome to the U.S. baby; the land of the fucking free," Ceazia spat back.

Judah shook his head while cracking a small grin, allowing a small peep of his dimple to show while showing his perfect white teeth. "Lata," he said as he got into his car and started it up.

"Bye," Ceazia and Diamond said in unison, and then stepped away from the car.

The beautiful visual before them disappeared as Judah let up the black-tinted window. Once the window was up, it appeared as though the girls were looking at themselves in a mirror; all they saw was their reflection. Judah blasted the tunes of Tony Matterhorn, "Nuh Fren We" as he sped off; leaving nothing but the smell of burnt rubber and the sight of the word MAGNUM in gold letters on the back of the car that had the state of Florida tags with the word TROJAN written across them.

"Trojan? Magnum? Black and gold? Oh, is it really like that?" Diamond asked, comprehending the hidden message within the coordination of Judah's car and tag.

"So I've heard," Ceazia said, licking her lips. "But I am definitely trying to get a taste." She thought for a moment. "I noticed that he had Florida tags. I wonder if that's where he's living now. Looks like he's doing big things," Ceazia said aloud, not missing a beat and taking note of every detail.

"Yeah, and it looks like you're being watched," Diamond said, noticing Shawn now staring from afar. Shawn stood near the club door chatting with a couple of his boys.

"For real? Who, girl?" Ceazia asked looking from left to right, anxious to know what other hopeless prey wandered near.

Without saying a word, Diamond cut her eyes in the direction of Shawn and gave her head a slight nod in the same direction in an attempt to look inconspicuous. Noticing Shawn was now walking in their direction; Ceazia pretended not to even see him and started talking to Diamond as if they hadn't just been plotting on him.

"Yeah, girl, the club was nice," Ceazia began with a general subject.

"Excuse me," Shawn said, interrupting their fictitious conversation.

"Oh, hi?" Ceazia pretended to be surprised by his arrival.

"What up?" He responded to Ceazia, then looked over to Diamond and held out his hand to her. "Hello, gorgeous. You are?"

"Me?" Diamond asked, sincerely surprised by Shawn's comment. She had been certain that he had made his way over to spit game at Ceazia.

"What?" Shawn could sense how flattered Diamond was. "Why are you acting so surprised? You don't consider yourself gorgeous?"

"Well, I guess?" Diamond said, giving little credit to her tall, slim curvaceous frame. "Thanks for the compliment. I'm Diamond, but you can call me *gorgeous* if you like," Diamond responded with a wink, now getting comfortable in her exchange of words with the fine specimen before her. "What is your name?"

"Shawn," Ceazia responded before Shawn had the opportunity to.

Shawn cut his eyes at Ceazia and then turned his attention back to Diamond. "Like she said, I'm Shawn."

"Taken by Danielle Stevens, ex-girlfriend of the late, great Snake," Ceazia continued, obviously hating on the attention that the mark she had been eyeballing all night was giving Diamond. Especially since Diamond had used little, actually, no effort whatsoever to get him to look her way.

"Damn, you sure do know a lot," Shawn said to Ceazia. "Although you probably don't know half as much about me that I know about you, ma," Shawn spat back, finally giving Ceazia one tenth of the attention she'd begged for all night.

"Wanna bet? I love a challenge," Ceazia dared Shawn in a childish manner.

"Nah, I'll pass on the game of trivia." He declined her offer, eyeballing Diamond from head to toe the entire time. "But as for you, Lady Di, I would hardly mind a game of twenty-one questions with you." He grabbed Diamond's hand.

Diamond looked up at Ceazia, noticing her added interest in Shawn and the slight attitude she now upheld and pulled her hand back from Shawn. "No, I better not," she declined.

"Girl, go ahead," Ceazia said in a nonchalant tone as if she wasn't fazed at all by the little spark going on between Shawn and Diamond. Hell, she knew she could spit on it at any minute and put it out. But instead, she decided to allow the hand to play out. "Shit, if you don't, girl, someone else will. May as well keep it in the family," Ceazia encouraged Diamond.

Ceazia knew deep inside that Diamond was hers. And if necessary, she could steal Shawn right from under Diamond's nose. After all, this was her forte while Diamond had simply been a witness in training. So, passing over the reigns of Shawn, someone she hadn't gotten the chance to claw her nails into anyway, didn't seem like that big of a loss.

"Spoken just like the nigga you are," Shawn said sarcastically, referring to Ceazia's known conniving and deceptive ways.

"What-ever!" she spat back and then rolled her eyes. "Girl, just get his number and let's go before I have to snap," she rushed Diamond.

"Here, I'll give you my number," Diamond held out her hand to accept his cell phone. "That way if you're really interested, you'll call."

Shawn handed over his cell phone and allowed Diamond to enter and save her number in it. She then returned the phone.

"Aight, baby girl. I'll holla at you." Shawn winked.

"Bye," Diamond said as she and Ceazia turned to walk away.

Shawn watched the bounce in Diamond's plump ass as she walked away. Although he had one thing and one thing only on his mind, he couldn't help but think of hitting that ass from the back and watching it hop up and down on his long black johnson. He watched Diamond and Ceazia walk across the street and into the parking garage. Minutes later, they pulled out in a dark fuchsia baby Hummer H2 that resembled a Barbie Jeep, hence the words BLACK BARBIE perfectly written in script in the upper right corner of the back of the truck. It was as perfect as a tattoo on a stripper's ass cheek. As Ceazia and Diamond pulled off, Shawn headed to his truck and dialed the number Diamond had just put into his phone.

As soon as her phone began to ring Ceazia said aloud, "Who the fuck is this?" She looked at an unfamiliar number on her cell phone.

"Answer it," Diamond said as though she knew exactly who it was that was calling.

"Hello," Ceazia answered, full of attitude.

"What up, gorgeous?" Shawn asked from the other end.

"Nothing. Who is this?" Ceazia asked with even more of an attitude.

"Damn, it's like that? You gave your number to that many niggas tonight? You got to screen calls and shit?" Shawn replied.

"Again . . . who . . . is . . . this?" Ceazia spit out her words slowly, pausing between each one.

"Calm down, ma. It's Shawn."

"Shawn?" Ceazia questioned then looked at Diamond. "You gave him *my* number?" she asked her.

"Yeah. I knew how much you had been working on him so I figured there was another opportunity."

What? Oh, she must be tripping, thinking I need some help getting a nigga. I get anything I want including all men; single, married, engaged and/or divorced. And can even turn a gay man straight, Ceazia thought before taking the phone away from her ear and saying to Diamond, "Boo, I don't need your help. Trust me, if I wanted him I would have him. I don't need no hand-me-downs."

"Baby, I didn't mean it like that. You are beautiful and I know you can have anyone you want. I just didn't want any problems with us, so I gave him your number. I figured you'd work your magic and get him," Diamond said sincerely.

Damn, now I feel bad for snapping. Ceazia's heart softened. "You didn't have to do that." Ceazia now felt sorry for the hate and evil thoughts she'd had earlier while she watched Shawn flirt with Diamond. "Give me a kiss." She began kissing Diamond, completely forgetting Shawn was on the phone.

"Yo!" they both heard him yelling through the phone receiver as if he was on speaker phone.

Ceazia handed the phone to Diamond and instructed her, "Talk to your man, baby. You can work this one out. I got faith in you."

With those words of confidence from the player who wrote the rules to the game in the first place, Diamond took the phone from Ceazia. "Hello," she said in the sweetest tone she could muster up.

"What's up with the games, ma?" Shawn spat. "I mean, if you're not interested, it ain't nothing but a thang, baby girl. Just let a nigga know." It was obvious that Shawn was slightly annoyed by Diamond's little stunt.

"No, it's not that. It's just that C is my girl and I would never want to hurt her or disrespect her. She was checking you out all night. I mean, I thought I even seen you checking her out for a minute there, so when you stepped to me, I was a little caught off guard. I mean, C was even gonna holla at you a couple of times, but she was intercepted," Diamond tried explaining.

"Damn, it's like that? She got holds on you like that, ma, where you can't even holler at a nigga freely?" Shawn inquired, just to see exactly how loyal Diamond was to Ceazia.

"I mean, it's not a point of her having a hold on me," Diamond began to say.

"You ain't got to explain nothing to him," Ceazia yelled, interrupting whatever it was Diamond was about to say. "Yeah, I got a hold on her *and* her pussy. That's my fucking girl. So now what?" Ceazia continued to yell like her mind was bad.

Diamond had never seen Ceazia's jealous side like this before. Ceazia had been the most confident person she had ever met, so why now was she feeling threatened? But Diamond didn't want to sit there listening to Ceazia clown so she just decided to end the call. "Look, I'll give you a call later or you can call me . . . for real this time. My number is seven-seven-oh-five-five-five-nine-nine-nine-nine." Diamond quickly ended the call then focused her attention to Ceazia. "Baby, are you okay?

"I'm fine," Ceazia snapped.

"So why are you so upset and yelling and cursing? May-be I shouldn't talk to Shawn. Like I said before, I don't want it to ruin things between me and you." Diamond rubbed Ceazia's thigh then squeezed it tightly.

"I'm sorry, Diamond," Ceazia sighed, closing her eyes and then taking a deep breath. "I'm tripping. Do your thing."

"You sure?" Diamond asked, wanting Ceazia to reiter-ate her approval.

Ceazia opened her eyes and looked into Diamond's. "Yes, baby."

"Kiss and make up," she said as Ceazia pulled into their garage and put the car in park.

Ceazia gently slid her hand behind Diamond's neck, tilted her head and pulled her in close. Moments later, her mouth was full of the warm wetness of Diamond's tongue. As they kissed passionately, all Ceazia could envision was that same warm wetness between her legs. As far as she was concerned, that little minor squabble that had just gone down was over . . . but the night had just begun.

Chapter 2

"How did things go after I left?" Danielle asked as she kissed Shawn on the cheek after walking into the bedroom where he was just settling into bed after coming in from the club.

"Everything's straight," Shawn responded with a stretch, giving little details of his night at the club.

Dissatisfied with Shawn's response, Danielle decided to probe him for a little more information. She had a lot at stake and the last thing she needed was for this nigga to try to get secretive on her and shut her out. "So were you able to get things rolling? Is everything going as planned?"

"Danni, relax." Shawn addressed Danielle by her nickname. "I got this. You too anxious, baby girl. Shit not gonna happen overnight."

"Well, it needs to," Danielle snapped, then plopped her

swollen body on the bed and pulled out a clove cigarette. "These guys aren't playing with you anymore, Shawn. They want their money." Danielle referred to the big drug lords in which Shawn was indebted. "And frankly, I'm tired of being fucking broke."

Since moving back to Virginia, things just hadn't been the same for Danielle. After Snake's death, she had picked up and moved to Atlanta with the initial intentions to hunt down Ceazia and get revenge against her. But then she met Richard Anderson, her ex-fiancé and NBA star, and fell in love. She put her revenge against Ceazia on hold for Richard only for him to turn around and leave her standing at the altar two weeks pregnant with his child.

While in Atlanta, Danielle had managed to use all she knew about the street game to build her own little empire. She had it all: career, money, NBA star fiancé, and even a man on the side; but when she crossed the wrong chick, Angel Powell, her world came crumbling down faster than the Twin Towers. The rest was history, so presently she was looking out for her future.

Now back in Virginia, pregnant with Richard's baby with nothing to support her but the money she received from him for prenatal care and any extra dollars she managed to swindle out of him, her life was miserable. Everyday she woke in misery. Although, Shawn seemed to really like her and did all he could to help her out, there was just no satisfying Danielle Stevens. There was no way Shawn could ever provide the lifestyle she was used to. That was the life beyond any big-time hood drug dealer.

After Snake's death Danielle was forced to start a life of misery with Shawn. As Snake's supplier, Snake was indebted to him. But Ceazia had robbed him of every dime so that left Danielle to face the music alone. With no way out she agreed to engage in a relationship with Shawn. The love-lacking relationship quickly turned sour, forcing Danielle to take matters in her own hands. To make a long story short, she set him up and set him to prison then fled with everything he owned, leaving him indebted to a number of others. Shawn somehow was miraculously released from prison and the first thing he did was find Danielle. In a bind of her own and feeling like Ceazia was to blame; she agreed to work with Shawn to get his money back from her.

Shawn sat up and snatched the cigarette from Danielle's hand right before she settled it between her lips. Then he crumbled it to the floor with his bare hand.

"Even if you don't give a fuck about your own health," he spat, "you should at least care about your lil' shortie in your stomach."

"My baby is all right," Danielle said nonchalantly, waving her hand as if she was shooing a fly. "This small amount of smoke is not going to harm it. Right now you're worried about the wrong thing. What you should be concerned with is money, and how quickly you can get it. Maybe if I wasn't so stressed, I wouldn't be provoked to smoke," Danielle continued to complain.

"Look, Danni, you're not the only one stressed around here. I got my eyes on the prize just like you, ma. But I know that in order to get it, it's gonna take some time."

"Exactly how much time? I've been patiently wearing the same Gucci sandals and carrying the same Marc Jacobs bag for three months now."

"I see you winding and grinding up on the floor," the tunes of Snoop Dogg and Akon sounded from Shawn's cell phone, interrupting Danielle's never-ending complaining.

"Here's the first step to executing the plan," Shawn said as he recognized the ring tone he'd assigned to Diamond's phone number. "What up, gorgeous?" he answered, and then got up out of the bed and walked out of the bedroom. He made his way into the living room where he could speak to Diamond in peace, without Danielle glaring down his throat like she was a fucking dentist or something.

"Nothing much," Diamond replied. "We just got to the house. I'm going to smoke to take off this little tipsy edge I'm feeling from all that champagne and wine I drank tonight. Then, I'm going to take a hot shower and call it a night. But I just wanted to call you and apologize for earlier; you know, make sure we still cool and all."

"No apology needed, baby girl," Shawn said in a sincere tone.

"No, that whole thing with Ceazia was really crazy. She's really a nice person, she just has her ways."

"Baby, I'm not trying to cause no confusion or throw salt on you and ol' girl's relationship or anything, but just how long have you known this chick, Ceazia?" Shawn inquired. Based on how Diamond was talking and acting when it came to Ceazia, Shawn figured that there was no way she could know the real Ceazia; the one that had made a name for herself in VA. And not a good name at that.

"Well, to be honest with you, I haven't really known Ceazia long at all. I've only know her a little more than a year. I met her in my hometown of Atlanta and we've only been here in Virginia for a few months. Why do you ask?"

"I'm just checking." Just as Shawn had thought, there's no way she knew all there was to know about Ceazia. "The respect and the image you have of her . . ." Shawn paused as he selected the right words to say, "I ain't trying to knock your love or nothing, but I really don't think you know the real Ceazia Devereaux," Shawn said to intentionally bring about doubt in Diamond's mind, despite what he had said.

"Huh? Why do you say that?"

"Is Ceazia around you right now?"

"No, she's not. What's up, Shawn? All your little comments make it seem as though you are beating around the bush about something." Diamond hoped she was letting on to just how concerned she was about Shawn's attitude towards her girl. It was like he knew something she didn't. And with all the long nights her and Ceazia had spent together talking about each other's lives, she was sure she knew everything there was to know about Ceazia; everything that mattered, anyway. But still, she couldn't help but read between Shawn's lines. Was the Ceazia she knew from Atlanta the same Ceazia everybody else knew in Virginia?

"Look, do you know her past? Has she bothered to tell you why she moved to Atlanta? Do you know why she's so hated in VA? Ever wonder why she has no friends?" Shawn shot question after question.

"Well, I guess I don't really know much about her past relationships with all these nobodies in Virginia, but that's just why, because they ain't nobody. But I don't think that is important. Even if she does have a bad history here, people change. The Ceazia I know is loyal, ambitious, giving, and caring. And in a lot of cases, these qualities have been taken for granted," Diamond said, thinking back to how Parlay mistreated Ceazia.

"Aight, ma. I'm not gonna argue with that. I just want you to be careful. Keep your eyes open. You're a really sweet girl, but a tad bit naive when it comes to the company you keep. A person like you, Ceazia would tear to pieces."

Now Shawn had taken things a little too far. Ceazia was her girl and she wasn't about to just sit there and let him dog her out like that. "Look, Shawn, it really bothers me when you make those types of comments," Diamond responded, this time with a little bit of attitude.

Diamond didn't consider herself naive at all. Raised in one foster home to another, she knew all about different walks of life. Plus the little time she spent as a dancer at Magic City in Atlanta really opened her eyes to a lot. And even with all the drama she'd gone through in her life, she'd still manage to come out on top. She was strong enough to decide what she wanted out of life and go for it. So naive was not her at all. But she felt no need to prove herself to a man she'd just met an hour ago.

"I hear the 'tude, ma. And I respect your feelings, so I'm gonna chill. Plus, I know you ain't call me to talk about Ceazia nohow. So what's up with me and you? When can I take you out? I want to show you the area. Take you to some of our nicer spots."

"That sounds good. When would you like to meet?"

"Who's that?" Ceazia's voice traveled from the background and through Diamond's cell phone right into Shawn's ear.

"It's Shawn," Diamond responded right away.

"Tell him to bring us something to eat," Ceazia continued to yell.

"Are you hungry, baby?" Shawn jumped at the opportunity to be able to come over to Diamond's house.

"Well, yeah. Sorta. Do you mind?" Diamond asked timidly.

Being an amateur to the game, Diamond wasn't to sure how to act. Of course she knew how to make her money in the club, but how Ceazia gamed niggas was on a whole different level. She'd seen Ceazia talk a grand out of a nigga just in one phone call, but that was the work of a veteran. "You've got to fuck them mentally," Ceazia would always say. But Diamond needed to start small and a free meal was a perfect start. Although she knew if it was Ceazia she would say, "Fuck the meal," and she would be aiming for a Denny's franchise instead.

"Not at all. What would you like?"

Diamond decided she wanted an omelet to eat while Ceazia ordered a T-bone steak, cheese eggs, and Welch's grape jelly like she was the Notorious B.I.G. or something. Shawn grabbed a pen and then wrote down what they wanted. After letting Diamond know he'd be there in about a half hour, he hung up the phone and then headed back to the bedroom.

"And where do you think you are going?" Danielle jumped in Shawn's face as he got dressed and picked up his gun, money, and keys off the nightstand.

"I'm going to handle business," Shawn answered with authority. "You been hollering all night about being broke and me owing niggas. So I'm 'bout to work on getting us some money."

"Whatever. Just please make sure you stick to the fucking plan. Remember, this is business, not pleasure. Don't get the two confused." Danielle lit another Clove and pulled a long puff, rolled her eyes, and then walked out of the bedroom where she had been patiently waiting for him to get off the phone.

Shawn stared as her plump ass bounced with every step. He contemplated getting a quickie from Danielle before rolling out. *Damn!* Shawn thought to himself as he grabbed his penis and shook his head in amazement. *Who cares that Danni is five months pregnant? That ass of hers gets thicker with each month and that pussy gets wetter!*

"Don't even think about it!" Danielle shouted as she peeped around the corner one last time before entering the bathroom and shutting the door behind her. She already knew from the look on Shawn's face exactly what he was thinking. There was no sexing jumping off unless she wanted it. To Danielle, this was strictly business but every now and then she would let a nigga get a taste. Lately things had been so bad that the only thing that could get her wet was Shawn producing some money. Other than that, his chances were slim to none.

After getting himself together, Shawn exited the house and headed out to complete phase one of his plan.

Back at Ceazia's crib, Diamond finished up her blunt as she watched Ceazia prance around the house straightening up while completely naked. Just looking at Ceazia's perfect frame made Diamond's clit swell and nipples get hard. She took one final pull on her blunt, then got undressed. She lay back on the bed and slowly parted her legs. She slid her hands between her legs and drowned her fingertips in the wetness of her juices.

"Ahh . . . hash," Diamond moaned softly with each stroke. Her screams of pleasure immediately caught Ceazia's attention. Diamond smiled as Ceazia walked near. Never being the aggressor when it came to her and Diamond's lovemaking, Ceazia stood bedside her and looked at Diamond seductively. Diamond grabbed Ceazia's leg and pulled it over her. Ceazia knew exactly what to do. As though she was mounting a horse, Ceazia climbed over Diamond and straddled her face. With a hand on each side of Ceazia's inner thighs, Diamond guided Ceazia's moves. Ceazia's head fell back as she gripped the headboard of her solid wood sleigh bed. Within moments, Diamond's mouth would be filled with the sweet nectar of Ceazia and she knew it. Each stroke of Diamond's tongue was sending a paralyzing pleasure throughout Ceazia's body as her climax neared. And Diamond lived to make Ceazia cum.

From the first time Diamond saw Ceazia all she wanted was to make her cum but Ceazia always had her own personal agenda. She'd used Diamond from the day they met. She persuaded Diamond into having a threesome with her and her ex-boyfriend, Parlay, then turned on her when he enjoyed it a little more than Ceazia would have liked. But never giving up, Diamond still stood by Ceazia's side and when her boyfriend broke her heart Diamond was there with a sewing kit in hand ready to mend it. She stood by her, tighter than Thelma and Louise. Her love was strong, but the question was how deep Ceazia's love was.

Ding-dong! Ding-dong! The doorbell interrupted Diamond and Ceazia's intimate moment.

Diamond grabbed Ceazia firmly as Ceazia was attempting to get up to answer the door.

"Don't get up, baby. Make him wait," Diamond mumbled from beneath Ceazia.

Ceazia got up anyway. "Trust me; we'll have an opportunity to finish this up later. Right now it's business before pleasure."

Diamond got up and headed for the bathroom. Without even grabbing a robe, Ceazia went to the front door and opened it for Shawn.

"What up?" Shawn said, totally ignoring the fact that Ceazia was butt naked.

"This is what's up," Ceazia said, pointing at her naked body from head to toe and extending her tongue in a snake like motion.

"Ain't nothing the whole 757 ain't seen in the strip club anyway. Where Diamond at, yo?" Shawn asked as he brushed right on by Ceazia, sure to let her know he had no interest in her at all.

"Find her yourself," Ceazia said. She slammed the door and then walked away.

"Yo, Diamond!" Shawn yelled from the foyer.

He examined the house as he waited for her response. He stood on hardwood floors that led into a hallway toward the living room. He could see the eat-in kitchen with a bar that extended to the living room. To his left was a door that obviously led to the garage. To his right were stairs that led to a loft.

"I'm in here," Diamond called out from the bedroom.

Shawn walked through the foyer, through the living room and into the open kitchen, where he placed the food on the kitchen counter. From the kitchen he followed Diamond's voice to the master bedroom down the hall. Once in the room, he noticed Diamond was in the bathroom. He grabbed the remote and sat in a chair in the corner and made himself at home as Diamond showered. He could see the silhouette of her body through the glass shower door. He watched intensely as Diamond lathered her body. Ceazia stood unnoticed near the bedroom entrance and watched Shawn quietly as he drooled over the sight before him. Envious of how Diamond had Shawn mesmerized, Ceazia spoke to make him aware of her presence.

"Like what you see?" she asked him with a smirk on her face, still naked. "I'm sure your mother told you it's not nice to stare." Once again, Ceazia was obviously hating on the attention Diamond was receiving from Shawn.

Shawn didn't respond. Keeping his attention on Diamond, he didn't even look in Ceazia's direction. Noticing, once more Shawn's lack of attention towards her, Ceazia walked into the bathroom and entered the shower with Diamond. She hugged Diamond from behind, then cupped her breasts, one in each hand. She gazed at Shawn while she kissed Diamond gently on her neck as she massaged her breasts gently. Diamond let out a pleasing moan. Preferring to watch a "Skinemax" after-dark special instead of the show before him, Shawn turned the channel to Cinemax and focused his attention there. Needless to say, without Shawn's attention, Ceazia's motivation was gone and moments later she and Diamond were out of the shower and dressed in boy shorts and tank tops.

"Hey, Shawn," Diamond smiled at him. "Thanks for bringing breakfast." She gave him a nice, gentle hug.

"Anything for you," Shawn replied. "It's in the kitchen, but it's probably cold now." Shawn followed Diamond to the kitchen.

Diamond grabbed the food as everyone then made

themselves comfortable in the living room. With Ceazia joining them, soon the threesome began to chat.

"So tell me about you," Shawn said to Diamond, taking a bite of his vegetable omelet.

"I don't know where to start." Diamond blushed. "Well let's see . . . I'm a Scorpio, I love performing arts. I've been in and out of dance schools my whole life. Since a small child I would watch *Fame* and wish I could be like them when I grew up. I would dance every chance I got. I even graduated with a degree in performing arts from Georgia State University. Back in Atlanta I taught jazz and modern dance at a couple local recreation centers. Ultimately, I hope to own my own dance studio for underprivileged kids one day. So, what about you?"

"Nah, not me yet." Shawn smiled. "You ain't told me shit. I ain't into quickies. Make it long and sweet. I want to know the real. What makes you smile? What makes you cry? What are your fears? What are your deepest secrets?"

"Well, I can answer that," Ceazia interrupted. "I make her happy. Men make her cry and she's afraid of being broke. As far as secrets are concerned, that's a trick question. If she tells you, then it's no longer a secret." Ceazia looked at Diamond for approval. "Right, baby?"

"Nah," Shawn answered before Diamond could respond. "That's you. I want Diamond to answer."

"Actually," Ceazia started. "That's not me. *My* response would have been slightly different. Money makes me smile, nothing makes me cry, and I'm afraid of the effects of drugs because I've seen what it's done to the best of the best. And as far as my secrets go . . . I have none. All I've done is known, yet unspoken." Ceazia gave Shawn an evil look from the corner of her eye.

"Yeah, that's cool, C," Shawn said in response to the look Ceazia was shooting him. "But I already know your story. Right now I'm trying to get Diamond's. Cool?"

"Okay, okay . . . kids. No fighting," Diamond stated, noticing the tug-of-war over her between Shawn and Ceazia.

"Yo, your phone," Shawn said to Ceazia, noticing the constant lighting of the screen of her cell phone as it sat on the coffee table in front of the couch.

"'Bout time somebody making a booty call," Ceazia said as she picked up the phone.

"Damn right. 'Bout time someone show your ass a little attention so you can let me have a little quality time with Diamond," Shawn threw in.

"Whatever," Ceazia responded to Shawn then focused her attention back to her phone. "Who is this?" she said aloud while staring at the caller ID.

Her life in the streets had made her paranoid. She'd done a lot of fucked-up things and made a lot of enemies in her day and she never knew if and when it was going to come back to haunt her. But she was sure to have her guards up at all times, so if that day did ever come, she would be ready for war. Before, she ran with a clique that always had her back just as she had theirs but now those friends were enemies and she was a one-woman gang, the female Rambo.

"Answer it," Shawn encouraged her. The caller hung up before Ceazia could answer. "Call this number back and ask who this is," Ceazia said as she handed the phone to Diamond.

Diamond did as she was instructed. "Hello? Did someone just call seven-seven-oh-four-eight-two . . ." she began
to read off Ceazia's number. "Oh, one moment please."
Diamond handed the phone to Ceazia. "It's the guy from
outside the club."

"For real?" Ceazia said, knowing it could only be one
person.

"Um-huh," Diamond nodded her head.

Ceazia said nothing more. Her face lit up as she grabbed
the phone and ran to the bedroom to talk to Judah privately.

"Damn. I thought she would never leave," Shawn
sighed, glad to finally get rid of Ceazia.

"So where were we?" Diamond asked, hoping to pick
up where they left off.

"You were about to answer my questions."

"Oh yeah. Let's see . . . seeing happy children makes
me smile. Thinking of my childhood makes me cry. I'm
afraid of being alone." With Ceazia being out of the room,
Diamond finally had the opportunity to answer on her
own.

"That's cool. But you left out one." Shawn noticed that
Diamond had failed to answer the one question he was
most interested in.

"Yeah, I know. I'm not ready to go into that yet."

"Aight." Shawn respected Diamond's wishes.

Diamond and Shawn's conversation was interrupted by
Ceazia's loud laugh that traveled from the bedroom.

"Ha, ha, ha, ha! Boy, you so crazy!"

"Damn! This bitch don't quit. Can we go to your
room?" Shawn begged to get as far away as possible from
Ceazia.

"Ummm, that is my room. We share a room."

"You mean to tell me there's only one bedroom in this big-ass crib?"

"No, there are a total of three bedrooms, a study, and a loft," Diamond said without elaborating on all the details of the house. "We can go upstairs to the loft if you like."

Shawn followed Diamond upstairs to the loft.

"There. You happy now?" Diamond said as they sat down on the soft, microfiber love seat.

"Yeah, man. Your girl be killing me."

Diamond chuckled a little. "What's really going on with you and C? Two people who don't even really know each other can't possibly dislike one another so much. So come on, start talking."

Finally out of earshot from Ceazia, Shawn began to tell Diamond all about the real Ceazia Devereaux. Meanwhile, Ceazia was downstairs stirring up a little drama.

"So what made you call me?" Ceazia inquired.

"Me no know. Me just curious." Judah tried to speak his best English. "What's up wit ya gurl?"

"Oh God! Don't tell me you too. I'm sick of this shit!"

"Wha happen?"

"I was scoping on this dude, Shawn, earlier and come to find out he wants my girl, Diamond, and now you want her too! Well, you're just going to have to wait in line because he's with her right now!" Ceazia ran off at the mouth.

"Oh yeah? Me never fancy her. Me just wanna know how tight you and she." Judah questioned to see if things were as Shawn had explained.

"Well, like I said at the club, that's my girl."

"You love her more than money?" Judah inquired to see where Ceazia's head was at.

"What? What the hell you talking about, Judah? You know how I roll when it comes to my loot." Ceazia said exactly what he wanted to hear.

"Well, dat boy dere you say she chat wit owe me money. So if he and she are like dat, then you must can get some info on him for me."

"If the price is right," Ceazia said like Bob Barker, the retired host of the game show *The Price Is Right.*

"Of course," Judah said, knowing that Ceazia was about the dollar.

"Okay, well that's a bet. So what type of info you need? I mean what exactly are you trying to do?" Ceazia asked, eager to get on it.

"Right now me know him living wit Danielle, but me never really see her out. Anyting you can tell me right now can help."

"Well, then, you got bad timing because you must have just missed her at the club. But trust me; one thing I know how to do is set a nigga up. I got this. Consider your money collected!" Ceazia assured Judah she could handle the deal before ending the call.

Never the one to put all his eggs in one basket, Judah had to have a plan of his own. Shawn had owed him money for some time now and the heat was on him strong. Shawn had made promise after promise to pay and nothing come through. Now that shit was hot he all of a sudden had a master plan that couldn't fail. He'd planned to set Ceazia up and rob her for a change. Shawn was convinced from the way she was flexing and all the people she'd robbed, she had to have a stash someplace and he was going to get it. Feeling bighearted Judah agreed to give him one more chance; but in case he did fail, he was sure to have a backup plan. Judah's call came right on time. Ceazia's funds were getting lower and lower each night and she was waiting on an opportunity to get back on top. Happy that chance was finally there, she immediately started to put the plan in motion.

"Diamond!" Ceazia called from the top of her lungs.

"Yes, baby?" she yelled back from the loft.

"Come here."

"Yes?" Diamond was in eyesight a few seconds later after leaving Shawn up in the loft to holler at Ceazia.

"You get your man?" Ceazia asked.

"Huh?" Diamond was thrown by Ceazia's sudden change in attitude.

"Shawn. You got him wrapped yet?"

"I don't know," Diamond responded, still a little confused by Ceazia's bipolar personality.

"Girl, you tripping. Get up there and get your man." Ceazia smacked Diamond on the ass and sent her out the room.

"Bedtime?" Shawn asked as soon as Diamond reached the top of the stairs.

"Nah. She was just encouraging me to hook up with you. I guess she's in a better mood since she got that phone call."

"Oh, so that's what you were waiting on? Her approval? Come on, ma. I already told you how she rolls. On the real, she probably only wants you to holla at a nigga so she can get a piece of the action. She could, in all actuality, care less about your ass. You're just a live-in accomplice."

Diamond thought back to how scandalous Shawn had just told her Ceazia was. It was as if he had planted a seed of doubt in her head and was saying things to water it in order to make it grow. "Shawn, you've told me so much tonight and right now I'm really drained; mentally and physically. Hell, as far as I know, you may have something up your sleeve. Why would you tell me so much about Ceazia anyway?" Diamond began to question Shawn's motive.

"I already told you. You are a really nice person. You don't even seem like the type to hang out with a person like C. I mean, it's obvious you two ain't cut from the same cloth. I'm just really feeling you, that's all, and I don't want to see you hurt. But from this point on, I won't say nothing else about C."

"Good. Well, I'm about to call it a night."

"All right, sexy." Shawn stood up and gave Diamond a tight hug.

She walked him to the door and said good night. Everything Shawn shared about Ceazia's past ran through Diamond's mind as she walked to the bedroom.

"You get your man?" Ceazia asked as soon as Diamond hit the bedroom door.

"We had a nice conversation. I don't know what to think of him just yet, though," Diamond stated honestly.

"What? Girl, think money. Think clothes. Think jewels."

"So how was your conversation with Judah?" Diamond changed the subject.

"It was cool. We caught up on old times."

"Did he mention BJ?" Diamond quizzed to see how Ceazia would respond.

"Nope."

"So what made him all of a sudden change his mind and try to get at you if back in the day he wouldn't even give you the time of day?"

"Don't know, but I'm taking full advantage of the opportunity." Ceazia kept it short and sweet, sure not to share too many details of her arrangement with Judah. She figured it would be better if Diamond didn't know.

Diamond knew that Ceazia was too smart to fall into any trap she tried to set to get her to spill the beans. She was fishing for any indication that one word of the things Shawn said may be true. Diamond struggled with her thoughts as she lay down to sleep. The things Shawn shared about Ceazia were eating her up inside. For example, she couldn't imagine that Ceazia was the type of person who would do so many devious and conniving things to make so many enemies and to even lose every friend. Diamond thought back to the two girls Ceazia used to be friends with who stood at the bar at the club. Then she thought about what Ceazia had shared about BJ and Danielle. As much as she wanted to ignore it all, she just couldn't. It just made too much sense. It would explain why Ceazia suddenly left Virginia. It would explain why she had so many enemies, and it would explain a lot about that natural inner hustle she had. Ceazia had more street knowledge than any female Diamond had ever met. Diamond placed her pillow over her head as she tossed and turned in an attempt to shake the constant thoughts from her head.

"Baby, you all right?" Ceazia asked, noticing the trouble Diamond was having falling asleep.

"Yeah, I just can't sleep."

"Well, let me see if I can't do a little something 'bout

that." Ceazia slid her hand between Diamond's legs, caressing her clit between her fingers.

Diamond moved slowly in tune with the motion of Ceazia's hand. With each stroke the frustrating thoughts were replaced with pleasure. Once again Ceazia had done exactly as she'd set out to do. Her mission was accomplished. After a few minutes of ecstasy, Diamond's mind was free and she was off to sleep.

Chapter 3

"What the fuck is your problem?" Shawn said as he opened his eyes to Danielle angrily straddling over him, staring him in his face as though she'd spent the last hour just watching him sleep.

"This is my problem!" Danielle exclaimed as she jumped off the bed and grabbed the pair of Shawn's jeans he had worn the night before and pulled the pockets inside out. "These empty-ass pockets are the problem, Shawn! You probably spent every dime you had on that bitch?" Danielle balled the jeans up and threw them at Shawn's face.

"Chill, aight?" Shawn said, catching them before they could hit him in the face. "Yeah, I had to shell out a little change, but consider it an investment."

"Have you lost your fucking mind? Or maybe you've just forgotten that you don't have shit. If I'm not mistaken, nearly every dime that comes in here is from me. Shawn, I can do bad by my damn self!"

Shawn wanted to see some money coming in just as bad as Danielle but nothing was jumping for him on the streets. Every now and then he would get a pluck but he just didn't have a real connect that he could rely on to keep a continuous flow coming in that could put him back on top.

With her hands on her hips, Danielle continued ranting. "I'm tired of being fucking broke! You claim you're going to use this female, Diamond, to get me the information I need to set up Ceazia to get our money! Ceazia's little thieving ass robbed me of everything, money and livelihood, when she stole that money from Snake. As his girlfriend, that money was mine to keep, and as his supplier, a portion was yours too. Now that alone should motivate you to stick to the plan. But it looks like you're looking for ass to me." Danielle went on and on and on, yelling at the top of her lungs.

Shawn yawned. "You done?" he asked nonchalantly as he drug himself out the bed and headed towards the bathroom, brushing by Danielle as if she wasn't even standing there; like she had been nothing more than a figment in his dreams, or better yet—nightmare.

"Fuck you, Shawn!" Danielle spat. "I am no stranger to the game. Hell, I once built my empire off this shit and I can damn sure do it again."

"You sure about that?" Shawn said with a chuckle that was laced with sarcasm as he stopped in his tracks. He then looked down at her stomach. "It ain't easy for a chick to run game when she's knocked up. Don't nobody want no chick that's five months swoll."

"Yeah, we'll see. I'm going to the mall to find an outfit and then I'm going to D Frasier's tonight," Danielle threatened.

"Holla," Shawn said as he continued his steps into the bathroom. Then sat on the toilet to have his morning dump, leaving the bathroom door wide open to let Danielle know that her threats didn't mean shit, literally.

"Fuck you with your trifling ass!" Danielle said as she stormed out of the bedroom, snatched her purse, and then headed toward the side door.

Shawn let out a loud disgusting fart that damn near echoed throughout the entire place and then called out, "That's what I say to that . . . bitch!"

"I hate you!" Danielle yelled in disgust as she went to open up the side door. "I should have known you weren't a true hustler! You're full of shit is all you are!" Danielle continued to yell all the way out the side door and into the garage.

"Yep! I sure am," Shawn shouted back, even though Danielle was long gone. "But that problem will be solved in about five minutes," Shawn mumbled as he strained to drop another kid off at the pool.

After relieving himself of all the bullshit Danielle claimed he was overflowed with, Shawn hopped in the shower. The entire time he showered, all he could think about was Diamond. He realized after spending a few hours with her the previous night that she was even more innocent and naive than he'd initially perceived her to be. Although she'd seen a few things throughout her childhood and during the brief time she was a stripper, there was still a lot about dirt, grime, and testiness that she had no idea about.

There was one thing about Diamond that stuck out in Shawn's mind more than anything, though; being the type a guy that never liked to give up, Shawn indirectly probed a little more when Diamond refused to share her deepest secret. Just the fact that she stated she wasn't ready to share that *yet*, let Shawn know that he would find out eventually. He just hoped it was sooner than later. Shawn figured that it may have had something more to do with her childhood since she had mentioned that thinking about her childhood made her cry. Not wanting to pressure her, though, Shawn backed off the subject even though the curiosity was really eating him up.

After Shawn finished showering, he threw on a terry cloth robe he'd housed from his favorite spot, the Ritz-Carlton, and grabbed his cell phone to give Diamond a call. He flipped his phone open and noticed the time: ten o'clock sharp; he'd only had a few hours of sleep.

Damn, I'm tripping! Shawn thought to himself, realizing that he had not even been awake for an hour and he was already giving Diamond a call. *Come on, dawg. This is business. What the fuck are you doing?* Shawn attempted to get himself focused again. He knew this was all a game. Diamond was just the bait to get the fish. But deep inside, he was really feeling her.

Many a man who had entered the strip clubs Diamond used to dance at with the intentions of just watching broads shake their asses had found themselves in the same position as Shawn. There was just something about Diamond's personality that always managed to find the soft side in a person. It was still undetermined, though, as to whether or not Ceazia had a soft side.

Shawn dialed the first digit of Diamond's phone number. "Fuck dat. I gotta stay focused—money on your mind, homeboy. Money on your mind!" Shawn said out loud, then closed his phone.

Meanwhile, Danielle had planned a well-deserved day of pampering for herself. Her first mission was to collect a few dollars to carry out her plan. She took out her cell phone and called her to-be-born baby father's house phone.

"Hello," a female voice sang through the phone.

Shocked to hear a female, Danielle removed the phone from her ear and looked at the number she had just dialed on the phone's screen, convinced she'd dialed the wrong number.

"He—hello?" Danielle stammered after confirming that she'd, in fact, dialed the number correctly.

"Yes. Who would you like to speak to?" the female asked.

"May I ask who I am speaking with please?"

"Angel. And you are?"

Just then, the voice on the other end of the line became very familiar to Danielle, and at that moment she was able to put the name and the voice to a face. It was Angel Powell.

"Angel," Danielle said, full of attitude. "What the fuck are you doing at Richard's house?"

Angel was the now ex-wife of Jonathan Powell, Danielle's ex-lover from Atlanta. When Angel found out her husband was cheating with Danielle, she set out for the ultimate revenge. She slowly ruined Danielle's perfect little life by taking everything from her job to her soon-to-be-husband, most eligible bachelor in the NBA, Richard Anderson.

"Well, I guess that answers my question," Angel said with a smirk.

"Who is it, baby?" Danielle could hear Richard call from the background.

Danielle's stomach turned and she became nauseous and faint while her unborn child did cartwheels in her tummy. Memories of her wedding day flashed before her eyes as she tried to gather herself and contain from losing every bit of sense she had left. "This wedding will be talked about forever," were the words Angel said to Danielle right before the wedding that still haunted her. All she could think about was that evil underlying little look Angel had when she said those words that Danielle would have noticed hadn't she been so caught up in the wedding bliss. Danielle felt in her gut something wasn't right at that point, but she just brushed it off as wedding-day jitters. Till this day she regretted not taking more caution. Maybe if she'd beaten Angel's ass the first time she'd gotten an uneasy feeling, it would have saved her from experiencing the most humiliating day of her life.

"You sheisty bitch!" The words flew from Danielle's mouth uncontrollably.

"Everything I know I learned from you," Angel responded in a very calm tone.

"I knew you were the mind behind that whole wedding scene. You fucking home-wrecking, wedding-crashing whore!" Danielle spat through the phone line, wishing she had Angel right in front of her so that she could choke the life out of her. "You better thank God you're on the other end of this phone in another state and that we're not face-to-face!"

"Yo, chill with all the nonsense," Richard said from the other end of the phone. Angel had handed Richard the phone so it was him who got to hear all of Danielle's profanities. But she still had a few left that she directed at him.

"Fuck you, Richard," Danielle said, now in tears.

"Come on, Danielle, you made it like this. You had the world but you weren't satisfied. You wanted the entire universe instead. Did you get it, Danni? Huh? Did you get it?"

Danielle couldn't care less about addressing Richard's concerns. She only wanted to know one thing. "So now you are fucking that bitch, Richard?"

"For real, Danielle, that's not even your business. The only business we have is my child you're carrying. So what's up?"

"I need some money. My clothes aren't fitting anymore. I'm nearly squeezing the life out of my baby with these tight-ass jeans."

"Cool. I'll send it by Western Union. Anything else?"

"Yeah, I hope that bitch makes your life miserable!" Danielle said before she began reciting the tunes of Tanya Stephens, "*I hope you wind up lonely, can't eat, can't sleep, can't breath*" Danielle sang then hung up.

She always felt Angel had set her up and now she believed it even more. Things were just fitting together too perfectly. She thought back on the series of events that had taken place leading up to the wedding. *I was having an affair with her husband. She ends up working for me at the law firm, then I end up fired. She ends up being the secret wedding planner for my wedding and my wedding ends up being a disaster. And now she's with the man that left me. Hah! Imagine that!* Danielle had to laugh to herself. She'd been beaten at her own damn game.

It took no time at all for Danielle to arrive at the check-cashing place where she picked up the money Richard had wired. Like every other time she'd requested money, it was always there right away. After she gathered her money she jumped on Interstate 264 toward downtown Norfolk and hauled ass to MacArthur Mall. She pulled up to valet, handed over her keys and headed towards the mall entrance. She walked through the mall doors and headed straight to Dillard's. Just the thought of her being pampered totally relaxed her body as she rode the escalator to the second floor of Dillard's to the spa center.

"I would like the ultimate destination spa package," she said to the feminine male at the counter who was wearing more makeup than she had ever wore.

"Oooh, girl, I love that one too," he said with a twist of his wrist. "Me and my *friend* got one together last week." He proceeded to ring her up. "Your total is going to be three hundred and three dollars." The man handed out his hand to receive the money. "Girlfriend, you are going to just love the ultimate destination spa package. It's the works. It includes the detoxifying massage bath, body wrap, deep tissue full body massage, facial, hand and foot treatment, and a lunch to go with it; five whole hours of pampering!"

"Hey, the way I see it, if you're not going to do it right, then no need to do it at all, huh?" Danielle handed the clerk the money and then sat on the chocolate suede contemporary-style sofa where she waited to be serviced.

"Oh sweetie, you're expecting. I don't know if this will work for you," the clerk said, noticing Danielle's belly as she sat down.

"Excuse me?"

"The detoxifying bath and body wrap may pose a problem. Maybe we should change your package to a pregnancy pampering package." The clerk begin to adjust her package in the computer.

"Wait a minute. I have not agreed to anything. Just what does this pregnancy pampering package include anyway?" Noticing that she was beginning to get a little loud, Danielle quickly glanced around to see who all was in the salon that would normally be packed with sidity white women and gay men. She didn't want to give off the impression as the ignorant black woman. Luckily no one was around to notice, otherwise she would have been just another sister to fit the stereotype. She walked to the desk to quietly discuss things with the clerk.

"Well, let's see," the clerk paused. "Really, that package is not similar to the ultimate destination at all—"

"Ma'am, right this way." An over-tanned woman with obvious fake boobs came from the back and interrupted the clerk's statement.

"Jan," the clerk called to the woman, "she's pregnant so we're going to have to change her package."

"Yes, but I am not certain I am interested in the pregnancy pampering package," Danielle responded.

"Okay, no problem. Just come on back. I'm sure we can put together something that will work for you." Jan directed her statement to the both of them.

Danielle followed her to the massage room. It was dimly lit with fiber optics used to generate the effects of stars and the sound of a Zen melody played in the background.

Almost instantly Danielle began to feel relaxed. "This is nice," she said as she entered the room.

The massage therapist gave Danielle a robe and asked her to get undressed and lie on the massage table. Danielle did just that and the therapist returned soon after. Unable to lie on her stomach, Danielle laid on her side instead.

"I'm sorry, but I can't lie on my stomach. I hope it's not a problem," she said to the massage therapist, a little embarrassed.

"No honey, not at all. I give prenatal massages all the time. I told you, I'll take care of you," the therapist assured her.

Danielle felt completely relaxed as she received the massage that started with her left side. It was as though each touch released a bit of tension. She followed every touch of the therapist from finger to finger to complete hand and up to her wrist.

"AAAHHHH . . . oh yes . . . oh yeah . . . right there!" Danielle's relaxation was totally interrupted by the moans of a female in a room next to her.

"Well, I guess she's really enjoying her massage," the therapist joked to Danielle.

"Yeah, but it's interrupting mine." It was obvious in Danielle's tone that she was annoyed by the sexual moans given by her neighbor.

"Yeah, I know. These walls are just too thin. Just try to tune her out by focusing on the melody of the music and relax, relate, and release." The smooth tone of the therapist's voice actually eased Danielle's tension, and in no time at all, she was relaxed again.

Her mind began to drift. She thought about how a day at the spa had been a weekly routine when she lived in Atlanta. She missed the life she had there. She was tired of living in a constant struggle. Never had she lived the way she was living and she refused to start now.

Danielle quickly decided that this day would be the last

day she struggled. She'd built an empire in Atlanta. Danielle went from nothing to a NBA fiancé, a lawyer at one of the biggest law firms in Atlanta, a nice crib and car to match, and she was confident she could do it again. She thought about some of the resources she had at her disposal that she wasn't taking advantage of. She knew she could always swindle a buck or two out of Richard, but she needed something more.

Her reputation as an attorney was shot due to the scandal between her and one of the senior partners at the law firm in Atlanta. At this point she was too afraid, and more than anything, too embarrassed to even attempt to get back in the criminal justice field. With that said, she would definitely need a man who could support her financially to help her get on her feet because perhaps Shawn wasn't the man for the job. That way she could go after Ceazia herself. One thing all hustlers are afraid of is the police and that's exactly who she planned to use against Ceazia. Everybody hates jail and especially Ceazia Devereaux. So her plan was simple: blackmail. She would give Ceazia an ultimatum—pay her off or go to jail. Danielle would tell the police every detail she knew about Ceazia's involvement in Snake, Duke, and Bear's murders.

"Okay, hon. Time for your facial," the massage therapist said, notifying Danielle that her body massage was over.

Danielle followed the therapist to another room where a couple of white women lay with green mud masks on their faces and cucumbers on their eyes. She lay on her back and prepared for her facial as she reflected back to the argument she had with Shawn earlier in the day. *"It ain't easy for a chick to run game when she's knocked up. Don't nobody want no chick that's five months swoll."* Those infamous words Shawn spoke stuck in her head. She could only pray that what he had said wasn't true as she had every intention of leaving that spa and going out on a mission; a mission to seek out a man to support her. And this time, she wouldn't let it get in the way of her ultimate revenge against Ceazia.

While Danielle's day partly consisted of enjoying a massage at the spa, back at home Shawn laid in bed enjoying a massage of his own. He watched the porno titled *Super-Head* as he massaged his erect penis. The phone rang, interrupting his deep concentration, nearly scaring the hell out of him. He felt like a kid getting caught jacking off by his mother as he answered the phone.

"He—hello," he stammered.

"What's up, Shawn?" a beautiful voice said from the other end of the phone.

"Ain't much." Shawn paused then smiled at the thought of Diamond calling him before he had given into his feelings of wanting to call her. "Just watching some *Andy Griffith.*" Shawn grinned to himself as he quoted the words from Martin's stand-up comedy *You So Crazy* used to describe the act of jerking off, choking the chicken or whatever niggas were calling it these days.

"Oh yeah? How is it?" Diamond asked just to be asking.

"It's all right. You know they're all reruns. Same ol' shit, different day."

"Ha, ha, ha, ha, ha!" Diamond laughed hysterically. "You're so full of shit!" Diamond said as though she didn't believe a word Shawn was saying.

"Damn. That's the second time I've heard that today.

Now that it's coming from you, I'm starting to believe that shit may be true. A nigga may really be full of shit!" Shawn began to question his character.

"Whatever. Do you watch *Andy Griffith* a lot?"

"Nah, just when I'm bored. But that's enough about Andy, what's up with you saying I'm full of shit?"

"I'll get to that." Diamond avoided Shawn's question, then continued on. "So, you only watch *Andy Griffith* when you're bored, yet you've done it so often til the episodes don't even excite you anymore."

"I guess; but is me watching *Andy Griffith* really that interesting?" Shawn asked, confused by all the questions Diamond was asking about the old television show.

"Yeah, it is. So if it's not even exciting anymore, why watch it?" Diamond asked yet another question.

"I don't know, ma. Now that I've met you, though, hopefully I won't have time to get bored so I won't be watching it no more." Shawn spat a little game to change the mode of the conversation.

"Well, I would hope if you were chilling with me you would stop playing with your dick."

"Oh shit!" Shawn said, surprised Diamond knew what he was talking about the entire time.

"Guess I'm not so naive now, huh?"

"DDDDDDaaaaaaaammmmmmnnnnnn!! You had me going, ma. You got me . . . yep, you got me. One up for Lady Di."

"Dat's right. I've seen the comedy show where when Martin was masturbating he would refer to it as watching *Andy Griffith*."

"Yep. You on point, shortie." Shawn gave Diamond her due props.

"Yeah, that's right; so back to your comment. Who else said you were full of shit today?"

"Damn, you don't sleep on nothing, huh? You don't miss a beat. I see I'm gonna have to step my game up a little bit for you." Shawn attempted to avoid the question.

"Just answer the question, Shawn."

"Nah, it ain't nothing. Me and Danielle had a lil' beef this morning and she said I was full of shit."

"Oh yeah? What's really up between the two of you anyway?"

"It ain't shit for real, baby girl. We really deal on some ol' business shit. We have a little arrangement and lately she's really been on some shit, constantly complaining about loot and all. Basically she's just miserable and misery loves company. But I ain't the one to give it to her." Shawn tried explaining his situation the best way he knew how.

"Arrangement? I've heard that term used before. That must mean she gives up the sex and you give up the money. That doesn't sound like business to me. I know you've heard the phrase, *business and pleasure don't mix.*"

"You're right. That's why she's business and I'm trying to make you pleasure. So what's up?" Shawn ran game once again.

"So what about that baby?" Diamond asked.

"So what about it?"

"You know what. Is that your baby?"

"Ha-ha," Shawn laughed. "Hell nah! So now what? Come with something a little better, baby girl."

"No, it's cool. I'll give anyone a try. I'll give you enough rope to hang yourself."

"That's good enough for me. So can I start now?"

"The ball is in your court, Shawn."

"Cool, well I'm gonna come scoop you up." Shawn wasted no time.

"I'll be here." Diamond disconnected the call then rushed to get dressed.

"Where are you going?" Ceazia asked, noticing Diamond grabbing clothes from the closest and then throwing them on the bed in a hurry.

"I'm going out with Shawn." Diamond paused to see Ceazia's reaction. Noticing Ceazia's look of disappointment, she asked if she'd like to join them.

"No. I'm good. Go enjoy yourself," she fakely said. "Just don't get caught up in no shit!" Ceazia warned.

"Why you say that?" Diamond asked as she turned on the water in the shower and got in.

"Well, you know he has a girl." Ceazia walked into the bathroom.

"Yeah. We already talked about that. I don't think I have anything to worry about." Diamond quickly lathered up some soap and began washing her body with her hands.

"Okay. If you say so. I just don't want to have to fuck nobody up behind some bullshit," Ceazia said as she began getting undressed so that she could join Diamond in the shower.

"You won't," Diamond answered. She hurried to rinse off, turned off the water and then opened the shower door to get out.

"Damn, you couldn't wait on me?"

"I'm sorry, baby. I'm just really in a hurry." Diamond stepped out and began to dry off.

"Obviously," Ceazia said, upset that Diamond had broken the morning ritual of them showering together.

Diamond rushed and threw on her clothes and fixed her hair. She wanted to make sure everything was perfect. She was really excited to go out with Shawn. She didn't know what it was about him but she was starting to like him. Money was no longer an object. That whole hustle thing wasn't even her, anyway; that was more Ceazia's style. This was the first time that Diamond had even been really interested in a man. Women had always been her preference and men rarely stood a chance. Shawn had no idea just how lucky he was. Maybe if it wasn't for Ceazia insisting that Diamond talk to him, they never would have hooked up at all.

Diamond's cell phone rang as she perfected her makeup. "Hello?" She rushed to pick up the phone.

"Yo, I'm outside," Shawn said from the other end.

"Is that anyway to pick up a lady? Hell, you may as well have just blown your horn," Diamond snapped.

"Come on, baby girl. You know I'm not feeling Ceazia. I'm not trying to come to the door and deal with her." Shawn explained his actions.

"You may as well get over it. We're a package; you can't deal with me without dealing with her."

"So is that how y'all roll? If a nigga got her he has you too? Is that what you telling me?"

"Of course not, Shawn. We each can do our own thing. We have an open relationship. But every guy should know home is where the heart is and we think about each other before any nigga. Okay?" Diamond explained.

"Yeah, okay."

"So get in here. Besides, I'm not quite ready yet." Diamond hung up the phone in Shawn's ear.

Thirty seconds later there was a knock at the door. "Could you get that, baby, it's Shawn." Diamond intentionally asked Ceazia to answer the door to see how the each of them would act.

"What up, C?" Shawn said in the friendliest tone he could muster up.

"Hey, Shawn. Diamond will be out in a minute. You can have a seat upstairs in the loft." Ceazia led Shawn up the stairs and he followed behind her.

She turned on the lights and grabbed the remote, turned the wall-mounted flat screen television on, then handed the remote to Shawn. "Make yourself at home; watch what you like."

"Thanks." Shawn accepted the remote and watched Ceazia as she walked into one of the extra bedrooms upstairs off of the loft.

He watched as she plopped on the bed and grabbed the remote and turned on the stereo. The bedroom was in clear shot from the loft. The calming tunes of KEM played as she flipped open her phone and dialed a number. Ceazia noticed Shawn watching her every move and decided to use this to her advantage. She closed her phone and sat up on the bed with her legs open, allowing her robe to fall open and reveal her naked body. Getting a glance at her vagina, Shawn thought, *Damn, she got a fat-ass pussy*. He then focused his attention back toward the TV in front of him. He knew Ceazia was up to no good and wanted no parts of whatever it was she had up her sleeve.

"Ah . . . ah . . . ah . . ." Shawn heard Ceazia begin to moan.

He looked toward the room to see what was going on. He saw her lying on the bed stiff as a board as she called out. "Shawn, come here, please," she begged as if she was in dire pain.

Reluctantly, and much against his better judgment, Shawn went into the room.

"My leg. I have a charley horse. Please help me get up so I can walk it out," Ceazia pleaded, reaching her hand out to Shawn.

When Shawn reached out to help her up, Ceazia yanked her hand back pretending to reach for her leg, forcing Shawn down onto the bed. Shawn leaned over her and attempted to sit her up.

"Ah . . . oh God . . . Shawn . . . wait . . . wait . . . oh . . . please," she yelled out as he lifted her from the bed.

Once Ceazia was standing on her own two feet, Shawn exited the room and back into the loft, where Diamond was standing at the top of the stairs.

"You ready?" she said with little emotion as she looked past him and at Ceazia instead. Ceazia darted Diamond an evil eye in return that she wasn't sure how to read.

Shawn didn't know how to react. He had no idea how much Diamond had seen or what she was thinking. All he knew is that things really weren't how they looked. He didn't want to jump to any conclusions and just start explaining because he was afraid that would make him look guilty. Unsure what to do, he decided to feed off of Diamond's actions. She acted nonchalant about the situation, so he acted nonchalant too.

"Yeah, let's roll." Shawn grabbed his keys and they headed out.

*   *   *

Back at the spa, Danielle's day had flowed wonderfully. A day of pampering and relaxation was exactly what Danielle had needed to recharge her battery. She felt like a new woman as she walked out of the salon. For a moment she'd forgotten where she was and her weakened financial status. But even reality couldn't get Danielle down at this point. She was rejuvenated and determined to make some changes. She picked up her phone to make Shawn aware of her next move.

Not even two minutes had passed since Shawn and Diamond had pulled off from her house when his phone began to ring.

At first Shawn didn't answer, but then Danielle began to call constantly back-to-back. Being that Shawn was already in a sticky situation, he was hesitant to answer.

"Answer your phone," Diamond demanded.

"I don't want folks to start interrupting our time together," he reasoned.

"Well, from the looks of it, whoever it is—is going to keep calling until you do answer so you might as well get it over with."

Taking heed to Diamond's advice, Shawn finally answered his phone. "Hello?"

"Where are you?" Diamond could hear Danielle's loud voice through the phone.

"Taking care of business; what's up?" Shawn responded.

"Yeah, I'm sure. I just hope you come back with some money this time. Anyway, I was calling to let you know I'm going to D Frasier's tonight."

"Cool. Enjoy yourself, ma," Shawn said and then hung up. He refused to feed into Danielle's madness.

Danielle knew just as well as he did that the club was no place for a pregnant woman. He knew she was fishing for attention and he refused to give her the pleasure of entertaining the bullshit.

Ten seconds later Diamond's phone rang. "Hey," she answered.

"Hey. I just wanted to know where you guys were going; in case something jumps off I'll know where to find you," Ceazia said into the phone receiver.

"Let me find out." Diamond turned toward Shawn. "Where are we going?"

"DC," Shawn said nonchalantly as though he'd just said Norfolk.

"DC?" Ceazia and Diamond both said in unison.

"Yeah," Shawn responded as cool as a fan.

"What? I don't even have any clothes. When are we coming back?" Diamond asked in a state of shock.

"I got you, baby. Just relax. Let a nigga show you a good time." Shawn intended to spend every dime of the little money he'd gotten from a quick sale he'd just come across.

"Well, I guess I'm going to DC," Diamond said to Ceazia nervously.

"Umph. Whatever. Well, just call me." Ceazia was full of envy as she ended the call.

The first hour of their ride consisted of little conversation as the tunes of Jay-Z's new album, *Kingdom Come*, blasted through the speakers. Unable to bear another minute of the uneasiness, Diamond finally broke the ice.

"Are you going to talk to me at all during this trip?"

"Of course. What's up?"

"DC is what's up. What you got planned for us?"

"I figured we'd have dinner, club a little, shop a lot, and then have sex." Shawn smirked then looked at Diamond to peep out her facial expression.

"Great. Shopping, eating, and clubbing sounds fun," Diamond said, intentionally leaving out sex.

"Oh, I guess three out of four ain't bad. I had to try ya. It's the American way."

"You're so crazy." Diamond grabbed Shawn's free hand and then reclined her seat back to relax a little.

They spent the remainder of the three-hour ride chatting and laughing. Not one word of that awkward moment Diamond had walked in on earlier between Ceazia and Shawn was talked about. Shawn drove to the Ritz-Carlton in Georgetown and hopped out the car to check in. Diamond remained in the car, using this opportunity to call Ceazia. She could feel from their last conversation that Ceazia was a little uneasy about the trip, but Diamond didn't want to discuss it in front of Shawn.

"Hey baby," Diamond said as soon as Ceazia answered the phone.

"Hey. You make it okay?" Ceazia replied.

"Yeah. We're checking into the hotel now."

"Aight then." Ceazia wrapped up the conversation in a hurry as if she had something much better to do.

"What's wrong, C?" Diamond asked with concern in her voice.

"It's just that you know nothing about this nigga. You know nothing about the bullshit games niggas play. Hell, as far as you know, his girl could be in DC following behind his ass."

"Well, for starters, Danielle has plans of her own tonight. I overheard her telling him she's going to D Frasier's.

Next, I feel like we've spent so much time talking, that I know everything there is to know. I feel safe, C. No need to worry, baby." Diamond assured Ceazia she would be okay.

"Okay. If you say so."

"Aight baby. Gotta go. Shawn is signaling for me to come in. Love you." Diamond rushed off the phone.

The valet hopped in the driver seat and gave Diamond the valet ticket before she got out of the car and walked off. She followed Shawn to the elevator where they rode it up to the fourth floor where their Royal Potomac suite awaited them on the northwest wing of the building. Diamond was in pure amazement as she examined the oversized hotel room. It consisted of a bedroom, living room, formal dining room, a study, and sitting room with a fireplace. It was as though she was in a large apartment. The room was furnished with mahogany wood and state-of-the-art electronics that included a plasma TV. Although, Diamond had no intentions on sexing Shawn, the room alone gave her a sense of sexiness that just made her want to drop every piece of clothing and jump on top of him.

"You okay with this spot?" Shawn asked, noticing that Diamond was still standing in the middle of the floor with her purse in her hand.

"Oh yeah. I was just checking the place out. It's really nice."

"Relax, get comfortable. We'll go down to the Fahrenheit, the hotel restaurant, and have some dinner a little later. Then we'll hit a few stores in Georgetown, and at about midnight we'll hit the club."

"Sounds like a plan." Diamond kicked off her shoes and plopped down on the bed and cuddled beside Shawn.

He threw his arm around her, kissing her on the forehead. He then pulled her close as he flipped through the channels of the plasma TV. Diamond felt so comfortable in his arms. She exhaled and smiled at the thought of possibly having a man in her life for the first time; a man that she could truly have feelings for, instead of a get-quick money scheme she was forced by Ceazia to participate in. This was the first time she'd actually dealt with a dude on her own. Usually any contact she had with a guy was Ceazia's catch and she was just there for that extra sexual edge. But this time things were different. This was Diamond's catch and the ball was in her court. Being new to the game she didn't know how to be strictly about the dollars. It was easy for a cat like Shawn to toss a little game and sweep Diamond off her feet.

"Looking for *Andy Griffith?*" Diamond asked sarcastically, referencing the conversation they had earlier in the day.

"Ha, ha, ha. Very funny," Shawn said, sucking his teeth. "No need—I got you here." Shawn squeezed her tight as they fell asleep in each other's arms.

Chapter 4

After her hours of treatments in the spa, Danielle spent a little time searching for something nice to wear for later on that night. She decided to go with a cute little black trenchcoat dress, a cheap replica of the one Beyoncé wore in the "Ring the Alarm" video. Still haunted by Shawn's words, *"It ain't easy for a chick to run game when she's knocked up. Don't nobody want no chick that's five months swoll,"* Danielle was sure to select an outfit that could camouflage her stomach. That particular dress was classy. And with the appropriate corset, she figured that dress would do a pretty good job of hiding her belly. Danielle was sure once she threw on her burgundy open toe platform pumps and oversized burgundy Gucci bag, one could only assume her dress was nothing but the truth. Exhausted from a long day, Danielle decided to grab a smoothie to satisfy her craving. Then she headed home to try to squeeze in a nap before beginning her night out.

She was surprised to see that Shawn wasn't home. Normally his days were spent in the house and his nights were spent in the streets. She figured he must have been with Diamond. One thing was for sure and that was that he'd better be bringing in the money!

Danielle wasted no time preparing for her night out. Full of excitement, she threw on the tunes of *Irreplaceable* by Beyoncé. This gave her all the motivation she needed as she cleaned the house and packed anything in sight that belonged to Shawn and placed it in a box in the left corner of the closet. After cleaning house and putting everything he owned in the box to the left, Danielle ran herself a steaming hot bath. She lit some candles, poured herself a glass of wine and put on the relaxing tunes of Robin Thicke. This is exactly what she needed to conclude her wonderful day of relaxation. Following her bath, Danielle decided to take a nap. It was only seven o'clock; she had a couple hours to spare.

As though she had a built-in alarm clock in her head, Danielle woke up five minutes to nine. She noticed the red blinking light on her cordless phone indicating there were voice mail messages. She must have been in such a deep sleep that she didn't even hear her phone ring, which was set to go to voice mail after only three rings anyway.

"Yo, pussywool, dis here is da bigman, Badman!" Danielle heard as she listened to her messages. "For me to call you, you must know shit is real. Me not call again. Dis here is me last call!" Danielle listened to the threatening message.

That was it! That was the last straw. She'd had all she could take. Shawn had told her that he owed people, but this is the first time she actually realized how serious shit was. His issues had never been bought to the home front. She called Shawn to inform him of his final collections call, but she was unable to reach him. Shawn's phone rang and rang, but he never answered. She didn't even bother to leave him a message. She figured he'd find out sooner than later.

Freeing herself of the bullshit, Diamond wasted no time getting dressed. She struggled as she attempted to put her corset on backwards so that she could close the hook closures appropriately then spin it back around to fit properly. Once she got it on correctly, she looked great. It was well worth the struggle. She could only hope and pray the few hours she'd plan to wear the corset wouldn't crush her unborn baby.

Now that she had tackled the hardest task, she threw on her dress and headed to the bathroom to apply her makeup. Always aiming to look as natural as possible, Danielle applied a light M•A•C powder foundation and followed it with a couple of squirts of M•A•C FIX IT spray. Then she applied eyeliner and mascara and a tinted lip gloss.

"Perfect," she said aloud as she examined herself in the full body mirror.

Now it was time to tackle her hair. Since she'd left Atlanta, she hadn't been able to get her routine visits to the Dominicans so her hair was a task. With a prayer and a CHI ceramic flat iron she was able to tame it enough to last for a couple hours. Everything was in order and Danielle was pleased with her look. With spirits high, she threw on her shoes and grabbed her bag and headed out the door.

Danielle arrived at D Frasier's in no time. She noticed a small line forming as she searched for an open parking spot. Finally locating a spot in a totally separate parking lot, Danielle hopped out the car, took a deep breath and began her strut. As she walked towards the club she noticed she'd caught the eyes of a few gentlemen on the way in. Not wanting to seem too desperate, she ignored the few calls the men made in an attempt to get her attention. She fell into the line that seemed to be moving rather quickly.

"ID please," a uniformed sheriff asked once she finally made it to the front of the line.

Danielle handed him her Georgia driver's license and opened her purse as the sheriff searched through it briefly. With a nod of the head, the sheriff gave his approval and she walked in. Danielle quickly glanced around the club as she waited to pay her cover charge. The club reminded her of the many small lounges in Atlanta.

"Ten dollars, please," the young lady said as Danielle walked up.

Danielle quickly paid her then walked directly to the restroom. She gave herself a final look even before facing the crowd at the club. Satisfied with her look and confidence high, she left the restroom and headed to the bar. She waited patiently for an open area and possibly an open seat. She noticed a few dirty looks from a couple females but assumed it was out of pure jealousy and ignored it. After waiting over fifteen minutes for an opportunity to order a drink, Danielle decided to grab a table and wait for a waitress. She sat in a booth towards the back of the club near a table that was filled with a group of guys. Without being too obvious she scanned the group for any potentials. There was one guy that looked like he may be able to support the lifestyle she was aiming for. His table was filled with bottles of Rosé, every guy that passed him in the club stopped and gave him a pound, and girls were constantly around him. On top of that he was dressed in Shmack jeans, fresh white Pradas, and wore a diamond-filled necklace that laid flat against his perfectly white thermal shirt.

Planning her move precisely, Danielle waited for the waitress to come over to her and then ordered herself a pineapple juice and sent the young man she was plottin' on a drink. The waitress returned with her order in less than five minutes. Danielle paid the tab and then purposely looked in the opposite direction as the waitress headed over to give the young man his drink.

After taking a couple of sips of her drink, Danielle was interrupted by a warm body that had suddenly slid in the booth beside her. Then she heard a soft whisper in her ear.

"Thanks for the drink," the sexy voice slurred between an upper iced grill.

That wasn't one of Danielle's preferences, but at this point, she had to get what she could.

"You're welcome," she responded in a tone just as sexy.

She looked the young man directly in his eyes as she began her assessment. He seemed a bit young in age with his demeanor, obviously a drug dealer and quite flamboyant; yet he seemed trainable.

"So what's up?" he asked as he now gave Danielle that same assessment she had just given him seconds ago.

"Nothing much. This is my first time here so I'm just checking the place out. You come here often?" Danielle started small talk.

"Yeah, every week," he answered, noticing Danielle's

obvious attempt to cover her stomach with her arms like Janet Jackson did with that pillow in the video for "That's the Way Love Goes." With little tact he asked, "What's wrong, ma? You pregnant?"

His question threw Danielle off completely. She didn't know what to say or do so she froze. The next the she knew he was reaching for her stomach. She grabbed his hand quicker than lightning.

"Stop!" she yelled.

"So I guess that answers my question," he stated and then got up from the table and walked off.

"Yo, what the fuck you doing, man?" Danielle heard his boy ask him as he headed back to the table.

"Nah man," he replied to his boy, "I ain't the family man. Dat broad pregnant, duke!"

With broken spirits and completely humiliated, Danielle just wanted to run and hide.

"You need anything?" the waitress interrupted her pity party.

"Yeah, let me get some wings to go, please." Danielle decided to grab a bite and call it a night. The words Shawn spoke earlier in the day had come to pass. *I guess Shawn was right,* she thought as her eyes filled with water.

She grabbed the cocktail napkin that her pineapple juice sat on and dried her tears before anyone noticed. She looked at her watch; it was twelve midnight. She had only been there an hour and she was already leaving. What a shame.

Twenty long minutes later the waitress arrived with her chicken. "Ten dollars." She held her hand out for Danielle to give her the money.

"Here you go, sista," a deep voice spoke with an accent before Danielle could even pull out her money.

Danielle looked up with surprise. "Excuse me?"

"Me a take care of dat for you," the small-framed chocolate man spoke.

Danielle examined him from head to foot, checking out his close-fit Versace print shirt and tight-fit cream Versace jeans wrapped up with his cream Gucci sneaker. *Momma always said you can judge a man by his shoes,* she thought to herself and then gave him a nod of approval.

"Thank you." With nothing to lose Danielle accepted his offer to pay for her food. It was only ten dollars, but sometimes it was the actual gesture and not the price involved that let you know what type of man you were dealing with.

"Me name Pierre." He held out his hand to Danielle.

As quick as she was turned on, Danielle was turned off. She'd never been the type to be attracted to an island man because they were all either possessive as hell or just outright crazy. And after hearing that message left on her voice mail earlier in the night, things didn't look too promising for any West Indian man. Besides, she could never understand anything an island man said anyway.

"Danni," she responded as she shook his hand and rolled her eyes.

"Danni, aye? Why such a long face?"

"Look, I don't think we're going to get very far," Danielle said, cutting things short.

"You a mind reader? You predict the future?" Pierre said, not giving up so easily.

"I'm just not into West Indian men," Danielle continued with the cold shoulder.

"Damn. What happen? You had a bad case of Jamaican fever?" Pierre teased.

Impressed that this man actually spoke pretty good English, and that he was comical, Danielle decided to speak with him a little longer. Besides, at this point she really had nothing to lose.

"No, but I did get a very rude message from a Jamaican on my voice mail today. It was from the bigman, Badman, the fucking original Don Dada," she mocked.

Pierre gave a small chuckle then looked away as though Danielle had hit a nerve. "Oh, I'm sorry, is that your brother or something?" she said, noticing his actions.

"You really give me a hard time. What is up?"

"I don't know. I'm just not having much fun tonight." Danielle put down her guard for the moment.

"Well, maybe me can change dat. What's stopping your fun?"

"I'm pregnant!" Danielle just threw it out there. She refused to give another man a chance to diss her.

"Oh yeah? Let's see?" Pierre looked down at her stomach then continued, "You're having a boy."

"Yes I am!" Danielle said. "How did you know?"

"It's just a secret me learned back home. We look at certain tings and it make us know."

"Really? Like what?" Danielle asked, genuinely interested in his theory.

"Ha-ha," Pierre began to chuckle.

"What?"

"You damn Americans; you too naive. Tink about it, beautiful. Me have a fifty percent chance of getting it right, so me guessed. Dere is no secret my country has to predicting a yute's sex."

"Yute?" Danielle asked, not understanding his verbiage.

"Sorry. Me mean child."

"Oh yeah! Well this American hasn't even had her doctor's visit to determine the yute's sex yet. So the joke's on you." Danielle laughed.

"Oh, so you got me. Me glad to see you smiling." Pierre gently grabbed Danielle's chin and looked her in the eyes. "You have a beautiful smile. It's very selfish of you not to share it."

Damn! Danielle thought as her heart skipped a beat. She could feel her cheeks getting red. "I'm sorry. It's just that I haven't had much to smile about lately," Danielle explained.

"A woman like you should have no reason to frown. What could be so bad?" Pierre tried his best to speak proper English.

"Oh boy. Where do I start? In the past year alone I've been through hell and back again."

"So speak. Me got all night to reason." Pierre grabbed Danielle's hand.

They spent the next hour talking about the drama Danielle had in the past year. Before they knew it, it was last call at the bar.

"Well, I guess it's time to roll," Danielle said, wanting to leave out before the rest of the crowd to avoid traffic and congestion.

"Me guess so. But dis not have to end we night. Dere's an after-hours spot near the beach. We could go dere for a few," Pierre suggested.

Danielle shrugged her shoulders and then didn't hesitate to say, "Okay."

They rushed out the club and headed to their cars.

"Follow me dere," Pierre instructed Danielle.

They arrived at the club fifteen minutes later. She followed Pierre to valet and handed over her keys. On the ride there Danielle had thought about the time they'd just spent at the club. He wasn't exactly her type, but his conversation was just so sweet and maybe that's all she needed for right now. The things he said seemed so sincere and it was like he said all the right things. He made her smile and laugh. Danielle hadn't felt that way in a long time. If it was only for attention alone that he was giving her, the night with Pierre was well worth it.

"Dis is more of my type of crowd," Pierre said as he grabbed her hand and they headed straight to the door, bypassing all the people standing in line.

Pierre whispered a few words in the security's ear and they were in. Danielle was impressed, "You must be a regular here," she stated.

"The owner is a good friend of mine," Pierre responded.

"Oh really? How do you know him?" Danielle started being her inquisitive self.

"Business." Pierre tried to answer without sharing very much information.

"So what do you do?"

"Let's find a seat and me tell you all about me."

Danielle searched the club like a hound on a hunt trying to find an open VIP area. This was finally her opportunity to find out just how much Pierre had to offer. She prayed he would be that meal ticket that she was looking for.

"What about there?" she pointed to an empty area in VIP.

"Okay." They went over and sat down.

The waitress met them as they sat down. "What are we having tonight?" she asked as she laid down napkins in front of them.

"Guinness and a pineapple juice, please," Pierre ordered, taking note that pineapple juice was what Danielle had been drinking earlier at D Fraiser's.

"So tell me, what is it that you do?" Danielle asked her question again.

"Me guess now it's my turn, huh?" Pierre responded, not too excited about his chance at trivia.

"It sure is!" Danielle answered, eager to know more about him.

"Well, me have me own business. Me guess you can say me is an entrepreneur."

"What kind of business?" Danielle fished for more information.

Hesitant to let Danielle in on his life as a big drug trafficker, Pierre continued to beat around the bush. "Imports and exports—kind of like the trade business," he lied.

"What type of goods?" Danielle was not giving up so easy. She needed to know exactly how many dollars he was pulling in. With any luck he could be the one she'd been looking for.

"Just major products from my country that your country has a great need for," Pierre answered, already aggravated by Danielle's persistence.

"Oh, okay. That sounds pretty interesting. Is that a pretty lucrative business?" she asked, getting right to the point.

"Ha-ha-ha!" Pierre laughed. He found it pretty funny that she would ask that question. "Yeah, it is pretty lucra-

tive, but sometimes you give men some tings on consignment and they never pay." He had a very serious look on
his face; almost as if Danielle was one of those people who
never pay.

"Consignment? Well, how would that work? That doesn't
seem like it would be very profitable." Danielle continued
her probing.

"Trust me, my girl. Me do good." Pierre laughed again
as he shook his head. The amount of money he made in
one week alone was probably more than some Americans
made in an entire year.

"What's so funny? I really don't understand how that
would be profitable. Because like you said, people don't
always pay," Danielle said, still acting confused.

"Well, they will pay me for however much they can afford and if they are a longtime customer and me feel like
me can trust them, than I will front them the same amount
they purchased. In the end, it allows them to build a little
more money and they can purchase even more than before. Okay? Like I said before, me make a descent living. "
Pierre was still trying to hide his true identity as the head
of a big drug ring from Kingston, Jamaica.

"Oh, okay." Surprisingly, Danielle accepted his answer
with ease. She had heard enough to know that the jackpot
had stumbled right into her lap without her even seeking it.

"You know, me ready to leave. Let's go to the beach.
You mind?"

"Well, I guess it's okay," Danielle answered, this time
not so sure if she was making the right decision.

Pierre grabbed her hand and they headed out the
door. He waited for their cars then Danielle followed him
to a parking garage at the oceanfront.

"Come." Pierre directed Danielle to follow him.

If felt as though her baby was doing flips in her stomach as she followed Pierre to a lavish oceanfront hotel. Danielle froze in her tracks.

"What happen?" Pierre asked confused by her sudden halt.

"I can't stay the night with you."

"Me not want nuting from you. Me just want to take you up to my room so that you can enjoy the scene and listen to the sound of the waves. Me figure that is something not every woman can appreciate, but you seem like one who can." Pierre placed his arm around Danielle's waist and guided her toward the hotel entrance.

All of a sudden Danielle felt like this was a bunch of game Pierre was talking, but it sounded so good. She hadn't heard such nice things from a man in so long and she was enjoying it. So she went for it. She gave in. Besides, if she gained nothing else out of the night, at least it gave her an opportunity to stay out all night and get even with Shawn.

The elevator door opened to the fourth floor and they headed to room 406. Pierre wasted no time preparing the room. He walked right over to the sliding doors and opened them wide. Then he dimmed the lights and sat in the love seat near the door.

"Come, baby." He directed Danielle to sit between his legs.

They lay comfortably on the sofa totally relaxed as they listened to the waves of the Atlantic Ocean crash against the shore. Danielle prayed that her feet didn't stink as Pierre removed her shoes one by one and began to massage her swollen feet. Other than the many masseuses she'd visited, this was the first time a man had touched her feet.

Within moments she was fast asleep. Pierre slowly moved Danielle over to the bed and undressed her with ease, sure not to wake her. He noticed the tight corset around her waist and shook his head in dismay as he removed it. Once she was undressed he placed her beneath the covers and pulled them over her snugly. He then sat back in the love seat as he watched her sleep.

Danielle woke from the glare of the sun that peeked through the hotel room curtain. She glanced around the room looking for Pierre. He was nowhere in sight. She rushed to put her dress on, deciding to leave off the corset. Just as she had gathered everything, Pierre walked in from the balcony.

"Have some tea," he offered, holding a steaming cup before her.

"No thanks," Danielle said as she looked over the room one last time to be sure she hadn't left anything behind.

"You leaving so soon?"

"Yeah, I've gotta get home."

"Me sorry, but me can't let you go." Pierre grabbed Danielle by the arm and pulled her close to him.

"Pierre, please, I really must leave," Danielle pleaded.

"No!" he said firmly, "you not go nowhere! Me a kidnap you."

Danielle froze. She'd never heard Pierre speak in such a forceful tone or with such a deep accent. She didn't know what to think.

"Relax, baby. A joke me a make."

"Wow," Danielle said, painting on a slight smile. "You really had me going for a minute." She looked at Pierre for a moment who did seem a little disappointed that she had to go. "Look, here's my number." Danielle scribbled her number on a hotel notepad. "Give me a call later."

"Lata." Pierre gave her a hug before she exited the door. "You have no idea, my girl," he said as he removed the Glock forty-five from his waist and contemplated on his next move.

At any moment during her stay Pierre could have taped Danielle's mouth and confined her, but he chose not to. Things had gone exactly as planned. Diamond had given Ceazia the information she needed without even knowing, and Ceazia happily passed it on to Judah. Pierre was pleased that all the information he'd received from Judah was on point. Danielle looked just as he had described her and she was at the club just as he'd said as well. Sure, Pierre wanted his money from Shawn, but he thought that in the meantime he might actually enjoy Danielle's company. She wasn't bad looking at all. In fact, she would have been one of his choices of women if the circumstances were different. Pierre figured he'd hold off a little while longer before he made any move. Besides, he could tell that he already pretty much had Danielle wrapped around his finger. He peeped her weakness within the first hour they spent together. Pierre knew Danielle was insecure about her pregnancy. He knew she lacked affection and attention and although Danielle tried her damndest to be inconspicuous about her gold digging, Pierre also knew she was about the dollar. So he catered to her needs. Pierre could have her in his presence at the drop of the dime. This here bait was definitely secure.

Danielle's body filled with excitement as she pulled up to her house. She couldn't wait to see the look on Shawn's face when she walked in. She went inside and dropped her things at the door; purse, shoes, and corset. Her swollen feet couldn't take another step in those tight heels. She strolled into the bedroom barefoot, where she expected to find Shawn fast asleep. To her surprise, there was no sign of him. She figured that maybe he'd gotten so pissed, that he had decided to sleep in the other bedroom, so she searched there as well. Still no sign of him. The more she looked around, the more it looked like Shawn hadn't even been there since she'd left him on the toilet the day before.

"That fucking bastard!" Danielle screamed as she flopped down on the couch with her arms crossed. It looked like Shawn had beaten her at her own game . . . this time.

Chapter 5

"Rise and shine, Lady Di." Shawn woke Diamond with a kiss on her cheek.

"Oh God, my head." She held her head as she struggled to open her eyes. "I think I have a hangover."

"That champagne a do it to you every time. You were a soldier, though. I was expecting you to throw up." Shawn rubbed Diamond on the back.

"I know. I don't think I've ever partied like that before."

"That's what I was trying to tell you, baby girl. It's one thing going to the club, sitting in VIP being posted up, sipping on a couple bottles of Rosé and drinking Voss water . . . yadie, yadie, ya . . . then there is partying. What you did last night was party. You let lose. You danced, walked around, mingled, laughed, took shots; you really enjoyed yourself. That's all I wanted to do is show you a good time. Hell, anybody can take you to the club."

"You're right, Shawn. I can't wait to tell C all about our night." Diamond sat up and began to search for her cell phone.

"I don't know why you in such a hurry to tell her anything," Shawn mumbled as he walked into the bathroom to start a hot bath for Diamond.

"What? What is it with you and Ceazia?"

"Baby, can't you see it?" Shawn walked from the bathroom and sat on the bed next to Diamond after turning on the water.

"See what, Shawn? See how you and her go back and forth like two lovers?" Diamond spat, thinking about the scene she'd walked in on the previous day at the house.

"Come on. Are you serious?" Shawn couldn't believe the words coming from Diamond's mouth.

"Shawn, although I may not speak on certain things, it doesn't mean I'm not aware. Sometimes I just store it away and continue to observe a situation until I'm sure that it is as it seems; then when I'm sure, that's when things hit the fan. Okay?" Diamond jumped up and headed to the bathroom, brushing by Shawn.

"So what are you saying? Just come with it, Diamond." Shawn followed her to the bathroom and turned off the tub faucets.

"That shit that I walked in on yesterday! What the fuck was that about?" Diamond's eyes began to fill with tears of anger.

"What? Diamond, come on. That was nothing. To be honest, I wouldn't be surprised if that dirty bitch did that shit on purpose. She's been trying to entice me since that night at the club. Don't tell me you can't see it." Shawn watched as Diamond stepped in the tub and lathered her washcloth.

"So what happened, Shawn? What was going on? To me it looks like you all were right smack in the middle of making out until I stepped in and interrupted."

"What? I'm not even attracted to that gold-digging ho! In fact, I don't even like the bitch!" Shawn shouted in disgust.

"Don't yell at me!" Diamond shouted back.

"I'm sorry, baby, but it just pisses me off that that bitch has you so brainwashed. I told you from the jump that I didn't want to come inside because I know how poisoned Ceazia is, but you insisted. I was upstairs chilling waiting for you. The next thing I know, C comes by and walks into the bedroom. She sat on the bed with her legs propped open. Knowing that broad was up to no good, I immediately turned my head. Moments later I hear her yelling for help. So I go in and she says she has a cramp in her leg and asks me to help her stand up so she can walk it out. As soon as I stood her up I walked away to meet you standing at the top of the stairs. It was nothing, Diamond. I promise."

"If you could have only seen the eye she gave me before we walked away. It was like a warning or something."

"Or was it more of a, 'I hate you because I ain't you,' sort of look? Come on, Diamond. You can't see what she's doing?" Shawn tried his best to convince Diamond of Ceazia's envy. "I mean, does this chick really like you, or does she want to be you?"

"But, Shawn, she has no reason to be envious of me. Ceazia is beautiful; she has everything and can get any man she wants."

"Except this one. You said it yourself; she was checking me out in the club. She was even attempting to holla at me, but Danielle ruined that for her. So when I met y'all after the club and I was only interested in you, that shit fucked her head up. She's never had to compete before." Shawn washed Diamond's back as he explained.

"But baby, we talked about it. She gave me the okay to talk to you."

"Yeah, but knowing C, it was only because she'd rather use you as bait to reel me in than lose the catch. In order to understand any of this I'm telling you, you have to know the real Ceazia Devereaux."

"So tell me, Shawn. I'm all ears." Diamond stepped out the tub and began to dry off.

"It's really simple. Ceazia is driven by money. It's like I told you before, that night in the loft. She will do anything from lie, cheat, steal, and never to exclude kill, to get money. Therefore, she'd rather you talk to me that would give her another opportunity to get at me than to lose me altogether."

"Yeah, but she hasn't tried to get at you," Diamond said ignorantly.

"Yeah she has. She's been trying from the first night I came over. She answered the door ass-naked asking me what was up, but I ignored her and asked for you. From that point on it's been war. She's been straight cock blocking on me and you trying to have something," Shawn explained as he followed Diamond back into the bedroom.

"I mean, it's nothing for us to share a man, Shawn. So maybe she thought you would be down. That's why she approached you. To be honest, we were right in the middle of sex when you rang the bell. So it would have been right on time if you would have accepted her offer."

"You straight tripping, yo! Dead this conversation." Shawn pulled out a bag of weed and backwoods from the nightstand drawer.

"Fine," Diamond said with a sigh, throwing her hands up in the air. "What am I going to wear today?" She changed the subject and began rambling through all the bags of things they'd bought the previous day before having dinner at the hotel restaurant.

"Here." Shawn threw her the La Perla panty and bra set from the Nordstrom's bag.

"This is it?" Diamond said, expecting him to toss her a pair of jeans and a shirt.

"For now. If it was up to me, you would stay naked all day." Shawn watched as Diamond rubbed lotion on her thigh.

"Damn! You are so fucking sexy." Shawn's penis rose as he looked as her protruding pussy lips. "Let me lotion your back."

Diamond extended the bottle to him and then Shawn took his time rubbing the lotion on Diamond's back while giving her a little massage while he was at it. Her head dropped with pleasure. Shawn slowly moved his hands from her back to her breasts. He kissed her gently on her neck, careful with every move. Shawn slowly moved his hands toward Diamond's private area. He parted her with ease and slid his fingers between her lips.

"Shawn, wait," Diamond whispered.

Shawn paused on her demand. "What's wrong, baby?"

"I've never done this before." Diamond sat up and faced Shawn.

"What do you mean?" Shawn asked, confused. He knew that no way under the sun was this chick about to tell him that she was a virgin.

"I've never had sex alone with a man." Diamond looked away with shame.

"Are you serious?" Shawn grabbed her chin and looked her in the eyes. "You don't have to if you're not ready, baby." He kissed her softly on the lips. This explained why she was always trying to pull Ceazia into the picture. She was afraid to be with him intimately alone.

"I'm sorry, but I'm not ready. Please forgive me."

"You don't have to apologize. It's all good." Shawn stood and handed Diamond the underwear. He then rambled through their many bags to find himself, as well as Diamond, something to wear for the day. For him he grabbed a pair of Bathing Ape jeans and a fresh cream thermal shirt and wheat Timberlands. You can take the nigga out of New York, but you can never take the New York from the nigga. For Diamond, a simple Juicy sweat suit and matching Pradas. Nowadays, having every color Pradas was as essential as having a fresh pair of Air Force 1's, DC's, Uptowns, or whatever people were calling them these days. Shawn hated spending all that loot on gear, but he knew the old motto that it takes money to make money.

Shawn tossed the clothes on the chair. "We're gonna keep it simple today. We've got a lot to do; lots of walking and shit."

"Where are we going today?" Diamond asked as she began to get dressed.

"Well, we've partied and we've shopped. Now it's time

to do some grown folks shits. We're gonna check out the White House, the Lincoln Memorial, and all that shit."

"Oh okay, but—" their conversation was interrupted by Diamond's ringing phone.

"It's your bitch," Shawn said, reading the caller ID on Diamond's cell phone that read MY BITCH.

"Hey baby," Diamond said, happy to speak to Ceazia.

"Why haven't you called me?" Ceazia spat.

"I'm just getting up. I slept late. I had a hangover," Diamond explained.

"Oh yeah? Where did you go?" Ceazia inquired.

"We went to Club Love."

"Oh God! Here comes the hate," Shawn interjected in the background.

Diamond darted her eyes at him and put her finger to her lips as an indication for him to shut up.

"What? Why the hell did he take you there? He is so wack. Did you have fun?" Ceazia started throwing hate just as Shawn expected.

"Yeah, I had lots of fun, actually. I don't think I've ever had that much fun at a club before."

"Umph. Did y'all go shopping?" Ceazia went on to the next question.

"Yeah, we did."

"Where did he take you?"

"Umm, I don't remember the name of the place. Let me ask him." Diamond turned toward Shawn. "Baby, where did we go shopping yesterday?"

"Nonya-town," Shawn shouted loud enough for Ceazia to hear.

"Oh, he's trying to be funny and say none of my business. I already know it wasn't nowhere but Georgetown. Again wack!" Ceazia said.

"Well, baby, I'm enjoying myself. Today we're going to the White House and to see some of the other tourist attractions."

"What? He is truly fucking retarded! Who the fuck goes to shit like that? I don't think anybody from the whole seven cities that's visited DC has gone to even one tourist attraction." Ceazia laughed.

"Well, I'm excited. I'm gonna call you later, okay? I have to get dressed." Diamond ended the call before Ceazia could make her feel even more stupid about actually being excited about the things Shawn had on his agenda for them.

"So what did the hater say?" Shawn asked as soon as Diamond hung up the phone.

"She really didn't say much," Diamond lied, trying to avoid confrontation.

"I wasn't even on the phone, but I betcha I can tell you everything that bitch said," Shawn challenged.

"What did she say, Shawn? And can you please stop calling her *that bitch?*"

Ignoring the latter part of Diamond's words, Shawn proceeded to respond to Diamond's query. "She said you should have gone to another club, she said you should have shopped some other place and that it was wack to go sightseeing. Right?"

"Basically," Diamond had to admit.

"If you can't see that she is a hater, than you just don't want to. Okay, her club and shopping preference may be a little different than mine and that's cool. But she can't knock you for going sightseeing. Only a certain type of woman can appreciate something like that and that's why so few will be taken places like that by a man."

"Okay, okay! I hear you, Shawn. I guess I just don't want to believe it."

"Good! As long as you're hearing me." Shawn grabbed Diamond and gave her a big smack on the lips. "Now let me show you a time that only a mature woman could appreciate."

As they got dressed, Shawn grabbed his phone to check his missed calls. He'd turned the phone's ringer on silent to avoid any interruptions. He had expected to receive calls from Danielle throughout the night since he didn't come home, but to his surprise there was only one call from Danielle, but no voice mail, not even a text message. He'd thought that maybe he should give her a call to check in, but as quick as the thought crossed his mind, it left.

"You ready?" Shawn asked Diamond, noticing that she was fully dressed.

"Yep," she replied.

"Let's blow this joint." Shawn grabbed all the bags and checked the room to be sure they weren't leaving anything behind.

After doing everything on their list of things to do that Shawn had told her, their day had finally come to an end and it was time to head home. Exhausted from touring so many sites, Diamond fell asleep almost instantaneously after hitting the road. Shawn relied on the same tunes that had gotten him to DC to get him back home. He blasted Jay-Z as he burned the interstate. Every so often he would glance over at Diamond. She was so beautiful. Although he knew this whole venture was only to get at Ceazia, Shawn felt for Diamond in a way that he knew was not part of the plan. He finally had to admit it to himself: he wanted Diamond. He wanted to steal her from Ceazia; talk about ultimate revenge. But then again, he figured that Ceazia was so stuck on herself that she probably wouldn't even miss Diamond, but he wanted her nonetheless. It was something about Diamond that made her different from the average chick. She wasn't fussy at all. She didn't have that nagging factor like most females. She listened to him, yet she wasn't a pushover. Hell, she even made him laugh, and for the past few months, he hadn't found shit funny. But now, like a breath of fresh air, there was Diamond.

Diamond opened her eyes to find Shawn staring at her. "What?"

"Nothing baby." He directed his attention back to the road.

"Thanks for everything. I can't remember a time where I've ever had this much fun. I guess all men aren't evil." Diamond smiled and grabbed Shawn's hand.

Damn! Shawn thought. *And she even appreciates shit!*

That was it. Shawn had made his mind up. There was about to be a major change in plans and he was ready to step up to anyone who had a problem with it.

"This is just the beginning, baby," he told Diamond. "This is just the beginning." Shawn squeezed Diamond's hand and watched as she dozed back off to sleep.

Chapter 6

"Hello?" Diamond yelled as she opened the door to an empty house. "Ceazia?" She ran through each of the rooms in the house looking for her girlfriend.

Once Diamond realized that Ceazia wasn't there, she decided to call her cell phone.

"Damn, it's already eleven o'clock. Maybe she's at the club," Diamond announced, noticing the time as she opened her phone.

She dialed Ceazia's number and began to take her bags into the bedroom as she waited for her answer.

"Hello?" Ceazia answered.

"Hey baby. I'm home," Diamond said, excited to be back to see her girl.

"Oh yeah. I'll be there in a few," Ceazia replied with little emotion.

"Where are you?" Diamond heard the music in the

background, yet it wasn't loud enough to be music coming from the club.

"A little strip club off Diamond Springs Road," Ceazia said, hoping she would upset Diamond.

"Oh. Well, can I meet you there?" Diamond asked in the same excited voice as before.

"Nah. I'm handling some business. I'll be there in a few." Ceazia hung up the phone in Diamond's ear then focused her attention back to Judah.

"The bigman spent some time with Danielle last night. Pretty soon him will arrange for them to take a little trip to Jamaica. If me need anyting else me let you know." Judah updated Ceazia.

"So when will I get paid?" Ceazia asked, always concerned about the dollar.

"When me get paid, you get paid."

"Cool," Ceazia wrapped things up before heading home to Diamond.

Back at home Diamond was crushed and couldn't understand Ceazia's actions. She contemplated calling her back but decided not to. She didn't want to anger her more. She decided to roll a spliff to calm her nerves. She laid on the bed, content as she flipped through the channels on the television. It was as though every other channel was showing a steamy sex scene. Diamond became more and more aroused as she watched. Her desire to have Ceazia home grew even more. She couldn't resist. She decided to call her again.

"Hello?" Ceazia answered the phone in an agitated tone.

"Baby, I want you home. I miss you and I want you," Diamond begged.

"Diamond! I'll be there in a few. Please stop calling!" Ceazia hung up the phone in Diamond's ear again.

Diamond was so confused that she turned to the only other person she knew for an answer.

"What's up, Lady Di? You miss me already?" Shawn answered his phone right away after Diamond had called him.

"It's C. She's really tripping."

"So what's new?" Shawn said sarcastically.

"Shawn, please. I'm really upset."

"Okay. I'm sorry. Talk to me baby."

"Well, I was really excited to see her because we've never been apart like this since we've been together. When I got home she wasn't here so I called her and she said she was at a strip club handling some business and then rushed me off the phone. She didn't even want me to come up there to meet her. So I decided to have a smoke so that I wouldn't be so anxious. As I was smoking, I came across a few sex scenes that made me want C home even more so I called her back. This time she really snapped, then hung up on me. What's up with her, Shawn; since you seem to know her so well and all." Diamond fished for an explanation.

"Baby, you already know my thoughts on this. She's a hater. She's mad because you've been out with me having a ball. She may even be envious because I've shown you some things that she hasn't seen. Baby, you have to understand, someone else is making you happy besides her. She's not gonna be too thrilled about that. But as for that little horny problem you have; I can fix that for you."

"Not to be funny, Shawn, but I want some feminine affection," Diamond said with no shame.

"Why would you wait for that when I can give you the same pleasure without even being in your presence," Shawn stated confidently.

Like nearly every other nigga in the drug game, Shawn had his share of jail time. His years in the penitentiary had practically made him a phone sex professional. Hell, if there was a demand for male phone sex operators, he would definitely be the star player; the fucking boy six.

"Whatever, Shawn." Diamond took a long pull from her blunt and focused her attention back to the soft porn on the television.

"Just follow my lead." Shawn's tone changed to a soft whisper. "First, I need you to remove every piece of clothing you have on."

"One step ahead of you . . . next."

"Damn! Okay, put your phone on speaker. You're gonna need both hands."

Diamond did what she was told. "Okay, now what?" Diamond was eager to get started. The lack of sex plus the movie on the television was really taking a toll on her. She figured whether she did this with Shawn or not, she would have been doing it anyway, so she may as well see what he was all about. After all, an episode of *Andy Griffith* never hurt anyone.

"Now lay back and spread your legs. Close your eyes and softly caress your nipples with one hand. Rub them until they are standing nice and tall." Shawn paused, giving Diamond time to follow his instructions. "Now lick the fingers of your other hand. I want to hear the wetness on your fingers and then slide them between your legs. Put that same moisture from your fingers all over your clit. Wet your fingers again and wet your clit. Rub your clit in a slow circular motion. Now squeeze your breast with the other hand. Does it feel good?"

"Yes," Diamond moaned.

"Let me hear you moan."

"Ahh . . . ahhh," Diamond moaned with each motion.

Ceazia was met with the sound of Diamond's moan as she walked through the front door. It wasn't unusual for Diamond to masturbate, plus she could tell from their earlier phone conversation that she was horny. So she wasn't the least bit surprised when she heard it. She took her time walking to their bedroom.

"Is that pussy wet?" Ceazia heard Shawn's voice coming from the bedroom. She froze in her steps and continued to listen just to be sure she wasn't tripping.

"Yes, it's wet, Shawn. It's dripping, baby," Diamond said between moans. "I want to cum, baby."

"No. Move your hand," Shawn demanded.

"Please, baby. Please," Diamond begged as she moved her hips in a circular motion, wanting so badly to give her clit that final rub that would just send her into a pool of pleasure.

"What the fuck is going on?" Ceazia walked into the room, nearly scaring Diamond half to death.

"Nothing, baby." Diamond quickly closed her phone with hopes that Ceazia wouldn't see it.

"Oh, that's what's up?" Ceazia said, relieved that it was just phone sex and Shawn wasn't actually there.

"Baby, I called you earlier and told you I needed you home." Diamond walked up to Ceazia and placed her arms around her waist to pull her close.

"So, when you can't get it from me you run elsewhere?"

Ceazia grabbed Diamond's wrist and released her arms from her waist.

"No. What are you talking about?" Diamond grabbed a robe and followed Ceazia into the bathroom just as her cell phone started ringing.

"Your phone is ringing. I guess Shawn is calling back to finish what you two had started," Ceazia said sarcastically, and then turned on the shower.

"I don't care, C. All I care about right now is you. You've been throwing shade for a while now. What is up? Are you interested in someone else?"

"Nope, but you are." Ceazia got undressed and stepped into the shower.

"So, that's what this is about?" Diamond dropped her robe and got in the shower with Ceazia. "No one could ever replace you." Diamond turned Ceazia around and placed her hand behind her head and pulled her close. "I love you." She kissed Ceazia and then pulled her bottom lip with a gentle bite.

The wetness of their bodies combined with the heat and constant flow of the water was all Diamond needed to get her even more aroused than before. She tongued Ceazia passionately as she slid her hands down her back and fingers into the crack of her ass. With one hand she grabbed her ass cheek tightly, piercing it with her fingernails and with the other hand she caressed Ceazia's asshole. Their bodies moved in tune as the passion grew. Diamond could feel the moisture release from Ceazia. With her middle finger, she pushed softly. With each thrust Ceazia moved her pelvis forward, stimulating Diamond's clit.

"Ah . . . shit . . . shit," Ceazia yelled, filled with painful pleasure.

The more she yelled the closer Diamond got to reaching her peak.

"You gonna cum for me, baby?" Diamond asked, always wanting to please Ceazia first.

"Yes," Ceazia screamed now with Diamond's entire middle finger up her ass.

That was all the confirmation Diamond needed. She opened her legs wide and pulled Ceazia tight as she thrust her hips forward in a continuous circular motion. Seconds later they both released backed-up tension, fluids, and emotions.

After showering, Diamond was sure things would turn for a better. They dried off and got comfortable in the bed. She hugged Ceazia tight as they lay in the bed.

"So how was your trip?" Ceazia asked.

"It was nice. I've never had so much fun in my life!" Diamond said, excited to share details of her trip.

Diamond spent the next fifteen minutes telling Ceazia all about her and Shawn's little trip to DC.

"You sound like you are really feeling Shawn, huh?" Ceazia asked her next question.

"Well, he's really nice and this is the first time I've ever been truly attracted to a man. So, I'm not too sure how I feel," Diamond responded honestly.

"Exactly, so you might wanna slow it down a couple of notches. You don't know nothing about niggas, Diamond. You don't know how to recognize game; you don't know how to tell if a nigga is cheating; you don't know shit. Besides, this was suppose to be about the dollars, remember?

When you running game on a nigga you just tell them what they want to hear and make them feel like they are the shit but the entire time you keep yourself free of any attachments. The only thing you should be loving is his money," Ceazia explained.

"Well, that's your thing, C. I'm not really into that. I'm feeling him and I am sure the feeling's mutual."

"Humph! Don't be so sure." Ceazia rolled her eyes.

"What is that suppose to mean?" Diamond asked, knowing Ceazia was about to start hating just like Shawn said she would do.

"He was just trying to get at me the day y'all left for DC," Ceazia said in a matter-of-fact tone.

"Oh yeah?"

"Yeah. I was sitting in the room with my robe on and he kept looking at me. I guess after a while he couldn't take it anymore and he just came in the room and forced himself on top of me. I was struggling to get him off. It wasn't until he heard you coming up the steps that he freed me," Ceazia lied.

"So he tried to rape you?" Diamond asked, just to see how far Ceazia would take it.

"I hate to say it like that, but I guess that's what happened."

"Umph." Diamond couldn't believe how real everything Shawn said was.

"On the real, Diamond, that's not even the first time he's came at me. The first night he came over he was all on me. When I answered the door he was trying to feel me up and shit. That's why he was acting like a lil' bitch because I dissed him and told him he was here for you, not me."

"Umph," Diamond said again, not sure to how respond.

"That's all you got to say is 'umph'?" Ceazia said, annoyed by Diamond's lack of response.

"I mean, what am I supposed to say? If he's a rapist like you say why would you even let me go to DC with him?" Diamond asked.

"It happened so quick I wasn't sure what to do." Ceazia played the role as the distraught victim.

"Well, right now I don't know what to do. I'm not too sure how I feel. I'll have to talk to Shawn about this and hear his side of the story."

"Oh, so you'll take his word over mine?" Ceazia sat up in the bed.

"I'm not saying that, Ceazia. I just don't want to jump to any conclusions. Things aren't always how they seem. I'm a firm believer of the saying, 'believe none of what you hear and only half of what you see'," Diamond calmly stated.

"You know what? Do you, Diamond, since you so fucking grown now. I guess he gave you a little dick so now you gone off this nigga." Ceazia hopped out the bed and began to search for a T-shirt to throw on.

"If that's your way of asking if we had sex, the answer is no, we didn't."

"Whatever, Diamond. I'm sleeping upstairs, good night." Ceazia threw on a big T-shirt, grabbed her cell phone and headed out the room, slamming the door behind her.

Diamond just shook her head, not knowing what to think. Things were changing between her and Ceazia, but she had to figure out if it was for the better or the worse.

Chapter 7

As weeks passed, Shawn and Danielle had seen less and less of each other. They both pretty much knew the deal. It was obvious Danielle was seeing someone and it was just as obvious that Shawn was feeling Diamond.

"I guess I can kiss any chance of getting that money good-bye, huh?" Danielle started the usual morning argument.

It had become a ritual for them to have a heated discussion about money and not having any each morning.

"You don't get paid to guess, think, or interrogate me, so I'd appreciate it if you would just leave me the fuck alone," Shawn spat, sick of hearing the same shit from Danielle's mouth everyday.

"And I obviously don't get paid dealing with you either, but I'm still here, right?"

"Well, is that nigga you been chilling with paying you?

How about a job? Is a job paying you? 'Cause right now I'm paying yo' ass no fucking mind!" Shawn sat at the side of the bed in his boxers and pulled out some weed and backwoods.

"I know you're not about to smoke around me and my baby." Danielle just had to nag about something.

"Bitch, you don't give a fuck about no smoke. You smoke your goddamn self. I'm not trying to hear that shit." Shawn continued to roll his blunt, completely ignoring Danielle.

"You have no idea what I have been doing. When is the last time you saw me smoke?"

Shawn was baffled. Danielle was right; he actually hadn't seen her smoke in the past few days, which was very unusual for her as she typically smoked everyday all day. But rather than to admit that he was wrong, Shawn chose to remain silent. He looked up at her as he lit his blunt. That's when he realized he also hadn't noticed how much her belly had grown in the last few weeks.

"No comment, huh?" Danielle noted Shawn's silence.

Again, Shawn just looked at her in disgust and didn't say a word. It was like he couldn't stand the sight of Danielle. The more she argued and nagged, the more he gravitated toward Diamond. It made him appreciate Diamond even more. If it was up to Shawn, he would never come home, and every night would be spent with Diamond. It was only convenience that he came home the nights he did.

"Yeah, that's best. Just keep quiet. Don't say a single word," Danielle said as she walked in the bathroom to take her morning shower.

Taking advantage of the few moments of silence, Shawn pulled a few puffs and enjoyed the soothing feeling of his blunt before making a phone call.

"Yo?" Shawn called Diamond while Danielle was in the shower.

"What's up, baby?" Diamond replied.

"It ain't shit; just trying to get out the crib. What's up with you?" Shawn was hoping Diamond wanted to get up.

"Nothing much. Come see me?" Diamond said exactly what Shawn wanted to hear.

"I'll be there. Just let me jump in the shower real quick. You need anything?"

"No, baby. Just call me when you're on your way."

"Bet," Shawn hung up the phone.

He wasted no time grabbing something to wear from the closet. Then he grabbed a pair of boxers and headed to the bathroom.

"What the fuck are you doing?" Danielle yelled from the shower.

Shawn continued to ignore her as he brushed his teeth. He was sure she could see exactly what he was doing so there was no need for an explanation.

"You know what? It's better when you don't speak, anyway. You're a whole lot more attractive. All you need is some money and you may be able to make some poor desperate woman happy. So if the time ever comes that you get some money, just remember to keep quiet. With that combination, you're sure to get a decent girl. And by the way, that advice is free. And that's the last free thing you will ever get from me." Danielle wrapped her towel around her and walked out the bathroom, not expecting a response.

"Free advice is only worth as much as you paid for it—not a goddamn thang!" Shawn finally broke his silence.

Without even giving Danielle the opportunity to start

running her yap, Shawn blasted the bathroom radio and hopped in the shower. He was on his way to see his boo and not even Danielle could ruin that.

Just like Shawn had Diamond on his mind, Danielle had Pierre on hers. She felt confident as she threw on her velour Baby Phat sweat suit that did nothing to camouflage her belly. She no longer felt self-conscious about her pregnancy. Pierre assured her she was beautiful regardless. Once she got dressed she jumped in the car and headed toward downtown Norfolk to meet Pierre at the Waterside Sheraton to have lunch in the hotel restaurant, but not before she made a quick call to Ceazia.

"Hello?" Ceazia answered the unfamiliar number.

"Hello?" the female voice on the other end of the phone said into Ceazia's ear.

"Who is this?" Ceazia asked as she walked downstairs into her bedroom.

"This is your worse nightmare and I'm back to haunt you—let me rephrase that—to hunt you," Danielle said. Danielle was convinced by the way things were going with Shawn that nothing was going to jump off with the money, so she decided to take things into her own hands. But contrary to what they all thought, Ceazia had little money. In fact, she was on the grind trying to get her weight up just like everyone else.

"Who the fuck is this?" Ceazia asked, assuming it was probably some upset female of a nigga she had fucked.

"This is Danielle, the girlfriend of the late Snake; the Snake you robbed and killed," Danielle calmly said.

"Okay, so what the fuck do you want, Danielle, the girl-friend of the late Snake; the Snake I allegedly robbed and killed?" Ceazia really thought this call was over some dick now. Why would this bitch be coming at her out of the blue years later? It had to have something to do with Shawn. Yep, just like Ceazia thought, some dick.

"Fifty thousand dollars," Danielle responded.

"Yeah, okay. You don't even have a five percent chance of getting fifty thousand dollars from me, boo. Please don't hold your breath." Ceazia laughed, knowing what was in store for Danielle. If things went as planned pretty soon Danielle would be nowhere in sight and incapable of collecting any money.

"Yeah, but you have a hundred percent chance of getting locked up for a triple murder if I testify against yo' ass." Danielle spoke fearlessly.

The night of the murder flashed in Ceazia's head. That moment that she and Danielle looked at each other eye to eye had come back to haunt her. What Danielle said was true. She was a nightmare that had come back to trouble her. This talk had finally caught Ceazia's attention.

"Fifty thousand?" Ceazia commented as if it was a possibility, now second-guessing herself.

"That's correct, and you have two weeks to deliver." Danielle gave Ceazia time that she thought was reasonable to collect the money then she disconnected the call.

She was tired of fucking with her. Ceazia Devereaux was only getting two more weeks of being on her mind and regardless if she delivered or not, jail was still in store for her. Danielle knew Ceazia's past and knew she couldn't take any chances of her coming back for revenge.

"Damn," Ceazia said to herself as she sat on the bed and saved the number Danielle had just called from. "What the fuck am I gonna do?" She knew she had a little time on her hands, because she'd arranged for Danielle to take an unexpected trip to Jamaica but what she didn't know was how things would go down when she returned, and she wasn't about to take any chances. She would fuck with a chick's man, fuck with dealing drugs, stripping, and even tricking but one thing she didn't fuck with was the fucking police.

For the first time in years Ceazia's heart felt fear. She'd done a lot of grimy things in her day and never thought twice about it, but jail was one thing she couldn't fuck with. With this on her brain she didn't even have the energy to annoy Shawn. Ceazia thought back to the time she'd spent in jail behind Vegas and that was just not an experience she was trying to relive.

Danielle, on the other hand, couldn't care less if Ceazia's ass burned in hell. Feeling like some weight had been lifted off of her shoulders by making that phone call to Ceazia, and happy that things were finally falling in place and confident that she was on her way to the top, Danielle pulled up to the hotel valet and hopped out.

"Whagwon, baby?" Pierre greeted Danielle at the restaurant door.

"Hi, sweetie." Danielle had learned a few words from the constant conversations they had.

After entering the restaurant, they sat at a corner booth in the back. Pierre constantly looked at Danielle as if he was trying to figure her out. Danielle noticed his constant stare but decided not to comment. Actually, she kind of enjoyed the attention. After ordering their drinks, Pierre grabbed Danielle's hands and looked her into her eyes.

"Baby, me have to go back to Jamaica for awhile," Pierre began to say.

"I guess nothing lasts forever." Danielle lowered her head with disappointment.

"Not forever, but me can make it last longer. Me want you to come to Jamaica with me," Pierre said, surprising Danielle.

"Are you serious? Oh my God! When are you leaving?" Danielle asked with much enthusiasm.

She looked down and rubbed her pregnant stomach wondering if leaving the country would be such a good idea for a woman six months pregnant. *To hell with it,* she thought. *This is a once-in-a-lifetime opportunity and I just can't let it pass. Hell, worse-case scenario I'll deliver my baby in Jamaica.* She laughed, knowing the chances of her delivering early were close to none.

"Me leave today, but you can come tomorrow." Pierre dug in his pocket and pulled out six one-hundred-dollar bills and handed them to Danielle. "This should cover your ticket."

"Thank you. I'll go online and buy my ticket as soon as we leave. I've got a lot to do today. I got to get my nails done, pack, and what about my hair?" Danielle thought of everything she needed to do in less than twenty-four hours.

Pierre pulled off another three one-hundred-dollar bills and handed them to Danielle. "Is that enough?"

"Yes, more than enough. Thanks," she said, truly grateful.

Danielle could hardly eat, she was so excited. It had been a long time since she'd had that sort of treatment and it felt good to get it once again. As she played with her food, Pierre still was unsure of his next move. He struggled to decide if he wanted to just tell Danielle what was up and see if she could be an asset, hoping maybe she alone could get the money from Shawn, or if he wanted to get to Jamaica and just hold on to her until Shawn paid him. Totally relying on the information he'd received from Judah, he figured Shawn was getting money on the side and stacking dough instead of paying off his debt. Word on the street was Danielle was the closest thing to him and the way Pierre saw it, if you have someone's prize possession, they will go to any extreme to get it back. But little did he know, Shawn had no stack and if it came down to it he wouldn't spent two pennies on Danielle. She was nothing close to a prize or a possession.

"Come upstairs with me." Pierre invited Danielle to his room to buy him some more time while he thought things over.

"Okay." Totally geeked about the whole Jamaica trip, Danielle was willing to agree to almost anything Pierre offered.

They walked in the room, and like always, Pierre had a room overlooking the water. They could see the entire pier, even as far as Portside, the marina in the city across from Norfolk's waterside. Danielle made herself comfortable and took off her shoes. She reminisced back to the last time she was in the hotel with Pierre, hoping he would massage her feet again. Pierre turned on the television and flipped to a soccer match.

"You like soccer?" he asked Danielle as he got comfortable on the bed.

"Well, to be honest, I've never really watched the sport."

"Come baby." Pierre patted the bed beside him.

Danielle lay down on the bed next to Pierre and he started to explain to her how the soccer game was played.

She'd dated Richard for years and he never once took the time to explain basketball to her. That's what she loved about Pierre; it was the small things that made him stand out from so many other men. Danielle wrapped her arm behind his back, placed her head on his shoulder and snuggled up as they watched the game together.

"You know, baby. Me tink me a stay and leave wit you tomorrow."

"That will be great!" Danielle said, preferring that they leave together anyway.

"But one ting."

"What?" Danielle said, knowing unless Pierre came up with some really off-the-wall shit, she would be agreeing to whatever it was he wanted.

"Me want you to stay wit me tonight," he requested.

Danielle lifted her head. "Okay but what about me packing and preparing for the trip?" Danielle asked, concerned that she wouldn't be able to prepare properly.

"You can do it tomorrow." Pierre provided an easy solution. "We can catch a later flight."

"Okay." Danielle agreed, then snuggled up beside him as before.

They spent the next few hours just talking. Danielle felt like she could finally exhale as they talked. They talked about their families, goals, dreams, and aspirations. Pierre explained that he grew up in the slums of Kingston and was a part of the Tivoli Gardens crew, one of the wickedest crews in Jamaica filled with badmen. He really didn't want to speak about that subject much, but he did mention he was never going back there. Coming to the land of the free was an accomplishment in itself.

After talking, they ordered room service for dinner

and watched a movie. By that time, the mother-to-be was exhausted, so she jumped in the shower so that she could prepare for bed. Minutes later Danielle came out wrapped in a robe and got back in the bed next to a resting Pierre. He opened his eyes as soon as she slid beneath the sheets beside him. He rolled over, looked her in her eyes, and without a word, they began to kiss. Danielle's body shivered all over. His touch alone was sending her to another level. As fucked-up as it may be, Danielle's pregnant pussy had been dripping for too long and she longed to have someone deep stroke it. Knowing what was about to go down, Pierre removed his gun from his waistline and placed it on the nightstand then grabbed a condom.

"Me want to make you cum again and again," Pierre said as he turned Danielle over. "Dis may hurt a little but you will like it." He began to position her.

Danielle got into an all-fours position and patiently waited for Pierre's dick to pulsate her vagina. Instead he chose her butt hole.

"No!" Danielle shouted, squeezing her butt cheeks tight and moving up the bed, away from Pierre.

"Just try it for ten minutes. If it still hurts after that, me a stop. Try not to tense up," he explained.

"All right. You better not come in my ass." Danielle moved her body back down towards Pierre, closed her eyes and braced herself.

Her hands clenched the comforter as the head of his penis pressed against her anus. She closed her eyes and tried not to tense up as he squeezed her ass cheeks and spread them wide open. After he got a rhythm going that both of them could live with, he started massaging her clitoris. Danielle didn't know if it was just her extreme horniness or just the rotation of the Jamaican wind, but she was already at her peak. She was ready to bust all over Pierre's fingertips.

Pierre took note to Danielle's undeniable pleasure and used it as an opportunity to make things more intense. Minutes later Danielle came on the bed comforter leaving her mark and Pierre soon followed. They locked eyes as both of them were trying to catch their breath. Exhausted from such extreme orgasms, Danielle started drifting off to sleep. Pierre got up and went to the bathroom to clean himself up. He returned with a warm washcloth and started wiping down Danielle's body. She preferred another hot shower, but was still flattered that Pierre was so thoughtful. While wiping her down, he began to reveal a few things to her.

"You know me spend much time traveling from Jamaica to Florida. Dis here was the first time me visit Virginia. I used to do a lot of business here, but a while ago someone rob me for me money. Me wait and me wait to get me money, but it never come, so me figure me better get it me self. Me have a friend here who had some dutty gal that assured him she can make me get me money." Danielle's heart began to race and her stomach began to turn as she hung onto Pierre's every word. "So when this here gal say me can find the man's pregnant girlfriend at the lounge, me go dere to meet you. Danni, me is Badman."

Tears welled up in Danielle's eyes as she began to put two and two together. "Noooooo . . . noooooo!" she screamed as she punched Pierre in his chest again and again. He was able to grab her wrist and hold her tight. "How could you do this to me?"

"Me never want to hurt you. Me could have a long time

ago, but me wait. Me really like you. Me will work something out. Me just want me money, baby," Pierre said sincerely.

Danielle had really grown on Pierre and if he could have his way she would be someone that he would definitely place by his side. He could see right through her. All Danielle wanted was financial stability and to feel loved. Pierre knew she didn't have a heart of a hustler. Her innocence was too pure. Of course, money was no object and he knew all the right things to say and do to make a woman feel like she was a queen. Even if it wasn't love that motivated him.

Danielle didn't respond. This was too much for her. She cried and cried not knowing what to say, think, or do. She cried herself to sleep, not waking until the sun came up the next day.

"Good morning." Danielle jumped at the sound of Pierre's voice.

"What's so good about it?" Danielle snapped.

"Danni, me really check for you." Pierre explained he truly liked Danielle.

"Just tell me what I have to do to get you your money and in turn get you out of my life."

"Shawn owes me thirty thousand dollars. So how can you help me?" Pierre asked.

"I don't think I can. I don't even know what is going on."

"It's simple. Shawn has owed me for some time now and the time has run out," Pierre said calmly.

Pierre had left it up to Judah to collect since he was Shawn's original connect and things were flowing with ease. But when he started to pay less and less money and less often it raised a red flag. Pierre started to feel disrespected and decided to take things into his own hands. The bullshit had gone on long enough.

"I don't have that kind of money, and neither does he. So it wouldn't have made a difference if you kidnapped me or not, you probably still wouldn't have gotten your money. And to be honest with you, we're not even feeling each other like that. What you need to do is get to the root; the real cause of the madness. You should be after that shiesty, conniving bitch, Ceazia. She's the cause of all of this." The anger Danielle had for Ceazia for so long resurfaced.

"Wait. Ceazia? Dat's the gal dat Judah has been getting his information from."

"Ha ha," Danielle laughed in Pierre's face. "That sneaky bitch is probably robbing your ass right now."

"Right now she tink me and you on we way to Jamaica. But me might can turn tings around."

"Well, you should. She's the one that owes you. I can tell you exactly how things got turned around. Shawn was supplying Snake, my boyfriend at the time, with enough drugs to supply the entire city of Norfolk. When Ceazia saw how we were living, she just had to have a piece of the pie. So she set him up, killed him and ran off with one hundred thousand dollars of your money, Shawn's money, and my money. So you see, Ceazia is the bitch you need to be after, but instead you're working with the fucking enemy instead of the ally." Danielle's proper demeanor had turned straight gangster.

"Oh yeah?" Pierre was taken by Danielle's demeanor as

well as the shit she'd just shared with him. "Me had no idea. Dis fucking dutty gal!" He kissed his teeth.

"So now what?" Danielle asked, knowing that she'd just thrown Pierre a curveball.

"Me have an idea. Me have she come to Jamaica to meet me and me handle tings from dere. Me want you to just sit tight. Make her tink me still have a hold on you. Me gonna get me money and me a take care of you too. Then if you want to leave and never speak to me again, you're free to go." Pierre's heartfelt words slightly tugged Danielle's heart.

"As long as I can order all the room service I want," Danielle joked.

"Whatever you want, baby." Pierre kissed her on the cheek. "Me just need you to do some tings for me. First me have to take dis." Pierre grabbed Danielle's cell phone. "Next, you can't leave the room, and final, you can't call outside of the hotel. Me have Judah, me right-hand man, look out for you. Him right next door."

"Fine," Danielle sighed, now a little worried about the decision she'd just made to be on Pierre's team.

"Trust me." Pierre kissed Danielle once more and then gathered his things to head out. "Me promise you not regret dis. Me have to make a few calls, me soon come." He walked into the bathroom and turned on the fan and shower.

Danielle laughed to herself. She wondered if he was truly making a call or inconspicuously taking a dump. While he was in the bathroom it gave her time to think. She really needed to evaluate things to see if she knew what she was really getting into. She really liked Pierre as a person. When she looked at it, he was handling business. And it must have been something there, feelings for her, for him to tell her what was really up. And in the end, what would she be losing? At the moment she was up nine hundred dollars, and once Pierre got his money from Ceazia, she could have her cut. Hell, that was actually a hell of a deal. She'd been struggling with Shawn to get money from Ceazia for weeks. Now all she had to do was chill in a hotel for a few days and she would have the money at her fingertips with no effort at all. Sounded like a good plan to her.

"Yo Judah," Pierre called Judah while in the bathroom.

Judah was his right-hand man and he knew he could count on him to do just as he was told. For years he'd sent drugs to him to supply Virginia and this was the first time there had ever been an issue. He knew Judah was more than willing to rectify the situation.

"Whagwon?"

"Me doing tings a little different now. Me not trust dat little dutty gal you fuck wit. Dat bitch dere is the one that fucked the money up. Get her a ticket to Montego Bay. Tell her Badman want to thank her personally. Never mind telling her anyting about Danielle. She dere here, in da room. She gonna stay here for a few days. Keep constant watch on her. Me not tink she a do noting still, but keep watch." Pierre gave Judah his instructions.

"Alright," Judah agreed and hopped right on it, giving Ceazia a call.

"Hello," Ceazia answered her phone on the first ring, praying Judah had some good news.

"Da bigman send thanks. Him got da girl and him want

to thank you personally. Me have a flight booked for Montego Bay tomorrow," Judah told her.

"For real? Damn right. I'll be there," Ceazia said, excited to receive that news.

"Aright," Judah said, ending the call.

"Damn right!" Ceazia yelled again.

Judah's timing couldn't have been more perfect. She was sure they had Danielle and shit was definitely going as planned if the bigman himself wanted to thank her.

Ceazia had spent every minute since she'd received that dreadful phone call from Danielle doing anything she could to get her money up. She had racked her brain trying to figure out where she could get fifty grand from. She only had ten grand of her own stashed away and she knew that wasn't even gonna make Danielle think twice. She'd done all she could to get some money but shit just wasn't like it used to be. She even went up to the strip club to see what was going on but nothing was even jumping there. She knew dancing alone would never get her the money she needed but it would at least introduce her to a few ballers that she could trick with and eventually do what she did best and rob them. Back in the day it was nothing for her to get at a balling nigga and take him for everything he owned, but nowadays cats were just too paranoid, especially with a chick with a reputation like hers. Shit had come down to the wire and Ceazia was really hurting. She knew she had to do something and she had to do it fast. There was no way she was going back to jail.

But that beautiful phone call she'd just received from Judah was her life raft. She knew that it didn't solve the problem of Danielle still maybe running her mouth to the police, but one thing was for sure, there was no need to rush. Ceazia figured Danielle couldn't collect when she was being held hostage.

Relieved that she no longer had that burden over her head, Ceazia started rambling through her closet to see what she should pack. As she stared at her things she began to think, *What if these Jamaican niggas don't hit me off and this trip is supposed to be my payoff?* Being a devious chick herself, all types of shit began to run through her head. *I can't go for this.* Ceazia continued to think until she came up with a little side scheme of her own. Being a true hustler, it was nothing for her to devise a plan. First she thought about cutting Judah's nuts and intercepting to get the money from Shawn before he had a chance to. But then she knew from the way Diamond spoke that things were rocky between Danielle and Shawn. So it was likely that Shawn may not even pay or at least he wouldn't be in no rush to pay. Hell, this nigga couldn't stand her guts. If it was up to him, he probably would have had the bitch kidnapped his goddamn self. Then she thought about Danielle's baby father, NBA star Richard Anderson. Yes, he would be the one. He might not give a shit about Danielle, but that unborn baby was another thing.

It was official. Ceazia was gonna do her own thing and cut everybody out of the deal. She would just have to deal with the consequences later. She began by doing a little research to get all the information she needed to make her plan flow smoothly. Once she got all the information she needed she wasted no time putting her plan to action.

"Hello?" a female voice answered the phone of the number Ceazia had just dialed.

"Richard Anderson, please," Ceazia said in her most

professional voice. "This is Ashley Bennet calling from his agent's office." Ceazia chose her words carefully.

"One moment," the female voice said then called Richard to the phone.

"Hello, this is Richard," he said.

"Richard, if you would like to ever see the birth of your child, I suggest you deposit twenty-five thousand dollars into Bank of America account number oh-four-oh-one-one-two-three-four-five and another twenty-five thousand into Chase Bank account number nine-eight-seven-six-five-four," Ceazia said quickly.

"What? Who the fuck is this? What the hell is going on?" Richard begged for an answer.

"For the last time, Bank of America . . ." Ceazia ran off the numbers to him again.

"Okay, okay the money is nothing. But how do I know Danielle is okay?"

"Send the money and you'll get your confirmation. Send me the money within twenty-four hours and once I'm sure there is no bullshit attached, I'll make sure you hear from her. Please don't try anything crazy. This is bigger than you know." Ceazia hung up the phone.

Knowing how things had been with Danielle since their breakup and aware of her past, Richard was sure her kidnapping was drug related. Fifty grand was change to him. He had gambled that away on one blackjack table in Vegas, but he needed to know that Danielle, the woman who was carrying his unborn child, was okay.

Richard decided to call her cell phone after speaking with Ceazia.

"Hello," Pierre answered the phone out of habit without even thinking.

"Hello?" A sick feeling came over Richard as the male voice confirmed what he'd just heard from Ceazia.

The sound of Richard's voice knocked Pierre back to his senses. Realizing that he'd just answered Danielle's phone, he immediately hung up and turned it off.

Richard called back repeatedly and each time the phone went straight to voice mail. After depositing the money, he spent the rest of the night calling Danielle and each time he went straight to voice mail. Richard left hopeless message after message.

Ceazia spent the rest of the day checking her accounts online. It didn't take long for Richard to deliver. Not even three whole hours had passed and she was fifty thousand dollars richer. Ceazia felt on top of the world. Her first instinct was to just take the money and dip, but the thought of being in jail again changed that thought with the quickness. She decided she would pay Danielle but it wouldn't quite be what she'd expected. For the first time in a long time Ceazia was back on top and she wasn't trying to let that go so easily. It was time to celebrate and her party would begin in Jamaica!

Chapter 8

As soon as the next day hit, Ceazia wasted no time before she was out the door. Diamond wasn't there when she left the house and she didn't even bother contacting her. She figured she was probably some place with Shawn. The vengeful side of Ceazia wanted Diamond to worry when she wasn't able to contact her. Ceazia arrived at the airport two hours early for her flight. She'd never seen so many people in one place at five o'clock in the morning. She stopped at one of the small airport stands to buy herself a Pepsi to calm her nerves. Since her trip to Cancún with Vegas, this was first time she'd gone out of the country. Many questions ran over and over in her mind. *I wonder where Diamond is. Does she even realize that I'm gone? Or is she so far up Shawn's ass that she doesn't even care? What is really up with these Jamaicans and this fucking big-*

man? Is he really a fucking Don Dada or what? The mystery of him is making me horny as hell. This seems too good to be true. But so was Vegas. So I'll take my chances. Ceazia was now confident in her decision.

"Ma'am, your bags please," the husky, hairy, Santa-like bag courier stated.

"Here you go," Ceazia answered, annoyed.

She was too busy checking off her mental list of things she'd packed and things she could have forgotten. *Booty shorts, jeans, shirts, summer dresses, numerous two-piece swimsuits to include string bikinis.* Ceazia recalled the clothing she'd packed then wondered on to underclothes. *Bras, thongs, G-strings, and lingerie?* The thought of lingerie lead her mind to other things. *Speaking of lingerie, this Mr. Bigman, whoever he may be, is going to have his tongue wagging between his ears when he sees me in my fire-red whole body piece with a hole where my soft pink lies.*

As fucked-up as it may be, Ceazia had been longing for dick since she'd left Atlanta. Diamond was cool and all, but Ceazia longed to have someone bang her hard; and if this Jamaican nigga was all Judah made him out to be, then he would be the perfect one to do it.

Ceazia's Victoria's Secret lotions were tucked away neatly in the left-hand corner of her navy blue Gucci luggage bag. And last but not least, she packed Trojan Magnum condoms. Not that she was concerned with getting pregnant, but very concerned with bringing something more than a souvenir back from Jamaica. She was only praying on the bigman's dick size.

Then she began to think of items in her purse that didn't meet the new airport security guidelines. She tried referring to the new three-one-one guidelines she'd recently seen on the news. *Three-ounce bottle or less; one quart-sized, clear, plastic, ziplock bag; one bag per passenger.* Then she began to think of things in her purse that didn't fit the criteria. The first thing that came to mind was her extensive collection of M•A•C lip glosses, foundation, pencils, and mascara in her purse.

"Excuse me." She flagged down the bag courier. "I need to put this in my bag." She began to dig out all sorts of items from her purse and empty them into her luggage.

There was no way she was taking the chance of having to toss those things in the garbage at the security checkpoint. Once she placed her things in her bags she checked them in and then headed through security to her departure gate.

"Are you all right?" the attendant asked as Ceazia was boarding the plane.

"Yes, I'm good. It's just that I'm not that good when it comes to flying. I'd much rather travel by car or train."

"Just try to relax. In a few hours you'll be in beautiful Jamaica."

"I'll try," Ceazia said, taking a deep breath and then heading for her seat on the plane. Once she was situated in her assigned seat, she reached for the iPod in her purse.

Ceazia had to admit that she was beginning to feel a little fucked up about her actions. There she was boarding a plan to Jamaica to be with the goddamn bigman, while Diamond was at home clueless and Danielle was being held hostage. That guilt only lasted five seconds when she began to think about that fifty thousand dollars she would be spending when she returned home. She realized the shit she was doing was grimy and she'd done it over and over again, but what the fuck does being a good girl get you anyway? She figured she'd take her chances, once again, at being a Gangster's Girl and wear the title proud.

To clear her mind of all the negative thoughts that were going through her head, she placed her earpieces in her ears and listened to some reggae to get her in the mood for her island vacation. Playing the reggae tunes made her feel a bit better. Resting her head on the plane window, Ceazia began to wonder about what the future had in store for her and Diamond, and Shawn and Danielle once she returned. There were many possibilities, both bad and good.

Bing, the bell sounded and the seat belt release picture lit up notifying the passengers it was okay to take off their seat belts and depart the plane.

"Whew!" Ceazia said as she departed the plane and walked through the many hallways to get to the airport immigration line.

She realized that the three-inch heels on her sandals were not the thing to wear. Her feet burned as she stood in the long line of Americans waiting to get through the immigration line. Although the fans and air conditioning ran constantly, the heat was still overwhelming. Relieved when she finally got her stamp of approval from the feisty immigration officers and after a thorough inspection from customs, Ceazia rushed out the airport, passing the currency exchange completely.

"You can't take that no farther, ma'am," a security officer said, stopping Ceazia at the airport door.

She looked at her bags, then looked at the young man like he was crazy. She gave a strong sigh then answered,

"Okay," once she realized he was referring to the cart she was rolling her luggage on. She was forced to take her two huge bags off the cart and carry them herself.

"Let me help you." An older man rushed over to Ceazia's aid.

Thinking back to the many stories she'd heard about Jamaica, Ceazia wasn't certain what to do. She was unsure if this man would take her items and make a run for it, or if he was truly there to help. Ceazia paused for a moment as she thought.

"Ma'am?" The man tugged at the handle of the luggage.

Ceazia's feet and the exhausting heat answered for her. It was as though they were screaming, "Yes, bitch, yes!" Ceazia loosened her grip from the bags and allowed the man to carry them for her. She followed him to a small area beneath an awning. There she sat on a bench waiting for the mysterious bigman. She noticed the man still standing there after she sat down and then it hit her. *Oh shit, he must be waiting for a tip.*

"I'm sorry," Ceazia apologized and then handed the man a ten-dollar bill.

"Thank you. Thank you," the man said gratefully.

Ceazia wasn't sure the difference in the value of the U.S. dollar versus Jamaican money, but from the excitement on the old man's face, she figured she'd tipped him pretty well.

Ceazia looked at her watch as she sat on the bench and waited patiently for her ride. The heat was so excruciating that Ceazia could feel sweat dripping from beneath her breast and down her thighs. And the craziest thing about it, she wasn't in the sun and she wasn't even moving. This was the driest heat she'd ever felt. She could feel sweat bead up on her upper lip and forehead as she observed the constant commotion around her.

"Baby . . . browning . . . empress," different men called out to Ceazia.

Finding it hard to understand anything these men were saying, Ceazia chose to ignore them completely.

"Yo, dred. My girl dat," she heard a male voice say.

"Hey." Ceazia turned toward the small-framed man, assuming it was the bigman.

"Whagwon, C? Badman," Pierre introduced himself.

"I finally get a name. Nice to meet you, Badman." Ceazia stood up and shook his hand.

The old man from before rushed to her aid again and grabbed her bags. He followed Ceazia as she walked with Badman to a pearl Toyota Sequoia. That wouldn't have been her choice of car, but comparing it to the many other cars around, it looked like Badman was doing it big.

"C, me want you to enjoy the country; but me a warn you to be careful. Dere are badmen and rude boys around and it's not safe. Dem boy dere see an American girl like you alone and you are sure to disappear." Badman began to warn her of the dangers as soon as they got in the car, which confirmed all of the rumors she'd heard about Jamaica.

"Understood," Ceazia nodded.

"Good, so let's have some fun," Badman said as he threw the car in drive.

"Where are we going?" she asked.

"Ssssh, don't ask too many questions. Just ride, baby."

* * *

Ceazia and Badman took a one-hour drive through the island from Montego Bay where the airport was, to Ocho Rios. The island was beautiful. The sights, sounds, and culture all intrigued Ceazia. On the route, Badman stopped at a small shack along the road and purchased a few mangos.

"East Indies," he said as he cut a piece of the sweet mango and handed it to Ceazia. "Your first taste of Jamaica."

They drove a little further then stopped at what Ceazia would describe as a wooden hut, but Badman referred to it as a jerk center. There stood a few men who cooked over a huge wooden grill.

"One small jerk pork with breadfruit," Badman ordered for Ceazia.

"Pickle pepper?" the man at the grill offered.

Badman shook his head and headed to a large wooden table big enough to seat ten.

"Your first taste of authentic Jamaican cuisine." Badman opened the foil, exposing its contents of pork and breadfruit.

Questioning just how sanitary some food cooked outdoors on a huge wooden grill could be, Ceazia was reluctant to eat it.

"Eat," Badman instructed, noticing her hesitation.

Ceazia did not want to be rude, so she forced herself to take a small piece of the jerk pork. "Umm," she said aloud, surprised that she actually enjoyed the pork.

Although the food was a bit spicier than she preferred, overall Ceazia really enjoyed her first bona fide Jamaican meal.

"So is this how you treat all women or is this special

'thank you' treatment that I am receiving?" Ceazia started small talk.

"Me know how to treat a woman, but the reason you are here is because me wanted to show thanks," Badman lied.

After eating, Ceazia and Badman visited an old woman near the restaurant who had a number of paintings and carved sculptures for sale. There Badman bought Ceazia a painting of three women gathering fresh water from a river. Their final stop was a beautiful rental house in a secluded area in Ocho Rios called Mammee Bay. Ceazia made herself comfortable as Badman brought in her bags. Waiting for an opportunity such as this one, she wasted no time taking off her shoes and relieving her feet of the pain she'd felt for the past few hours. She walked around the small home looking through each window and admiring the view from every angle.

"You not wait for me to tell you to make yourself at home, eh?" Badman asked, noticing Ceazia had taken off her shoes and given herself a tour of the house.

"I'm sorry, no disrespect. I'm just so used to doing my own thing and not waiting on anyone before I make a move," Ceazia said, wanting to show Badman that she was a no-nonsense chick just as much as he was a no-nonsense dude.

"Have something to drink," Badman said, choosing to ignore her statement while opening the fully stocked refrigerator and pulling out a Guinness for himself and a bottle of water for Ceazia.

"Thank you, but I would much rather have an alcoholic beverage," she said to reiterate her leader status, then laughed and accepted the water.

"What would you like to do next?" Badman asked, allowing Ceazia to flex a little while walking towards her.

"I would like to take a shower. I feel sticky between my legs," Ceazia replied, feeling a little self-conscious about all the sitting she'd done at the airport and all of the perspiring she had done.

"You do now," Badman answered back while playfully lifting up Ceazia's skirt. "Lets see?" He began to shift her orange thong to the side to see just how far she would let him go.

"Stop it," Ceazia laughed, then squeezed her thighs together enjoying the tease but still a little uneasy about the sweat.

"No, really me a tell you. Free yourself girl." Badman's accent alone was turning her on.

Wanting to be touched more than anything, Ceazia gave in. She did exactly as Badman requested and let herself free, allowing her legs to collapse open like she was preparing for a Pap smear and Badman was her ob-gyn. Taking that as an invitation, Badman used his index and middle fingers on his right hand and gently inserted them into the tip of her vagina.

"Yeah, you're sticky and sweet," he stated while rubbing those same two fingers against his thumb in a circular motion, feeling the consistency of the wetness of Ceazia's pussy then smelling it.

Ceazia pulled away; although she truly wished Badman would touch her again, only the next time it would hopefully be with another part of his body.

"After my shower I want to go to the beach," she said, knowing there was a secluded beach area right outside.

"Please give me twenty minutes in the bathroom," Ceazia said, needing a cold shower to offset the overwhelming horny feeling she was having.

She walked away and rushed into the bedroom and began fumbling through her suitcase while trying to keep her composure.

Twenty minutes had turned into an hour as Ceazia touched up on a few areas with her razor, washed and double-washed with her favorite body wash, and carefully placed lotion on every inch of her body. When she opened the bathroom door, she found Badman watching a soccer game.

"I'm back." Ceazia walked into the living room. She was dressed in a banana-colored two-piece G-string bikini with a matching wrap.

"You look gorgeous, baby." Badman admired her beauty.

It took Badman several minutes to return his eyes to the television. Ceazia could tell he wanted to say more but he held back. She sat down on the couch next to him and he started to explain to her how the soccer game was played. He ran the exact same game on Ceazia that he had ran on Danielle one day before. He figured what worked on one worked on all, and in this case he was right.

"Damn, I've never had a dude explain a game to me. Most niggas just want a bitch out the way when they are into their sports." Ceazia was impressed.

That little bit of attention made her pussy soak. She threw her legs over his lap and snuggled up close as they watched the game together. After the game they headed to the beach. The rest of their night was spent enjoying the air, the breeze, and the water.

* * *

For the next couple of days Badman treated Ceazia like a queen. And she had no idea what was in store for her. He figured what's a little time spent. Hell, it was nothing but a little change out of pocket and he actually was enjoying himself. Besides, he knew in the end he would get an awesome piece of ass and his money too. That alone was worth the time spent. He took Ceazia everywhere and visited all the tourist attractions. They climbed the mountain at Dunns River and they swam with the dolphins at Dolphin Cove. They partied with other tourists and a few locals at a popular club in Ocho Rios called Margaritaville. Ceazia even went to a couple true Jamaican parties. She attended a beach party, a Guinness party, partied at Club Asylum, and even went to a sound clash.

As the days were winding down, Ceazia had become pretty exhausted. Badman could see how weary she'd become and suggested they spend their final days enjoying each other's company at the house. Ceazia happily agreed, hoping that time spent at the house uninterrupted meant that sex was in store. She didn't know if it was the atmosphere, the setting, or just plain hormones, but it had become nearly impossible for her to maintain. She realized it was inevitable and accepted the fact she may have to make the first move. With that in mind, Ceazia began to prepare. She sprang from the shower naked and ran past a sleeping Badman and searched through her suitcase for the perfect piece of lingerie and then raced back to the bathroom. Ceazia put on her infamous fire-red body piece and topped it off with five-inch red stiletto heels. This time when she opened the bathroom door, Badman was sitting on the edge of the bed and couldn't take his eyes off of her. She walked seductively towards him. She stopped where at least three feet were between them. She turned around slowly so he could get the full effect of her body then bent over. Badman's mouth dropped as his eyes were fixated on her ripe, pink pussy. Right before he reached for her ass, Ceazia lifted up and turned back around.

"You're not ready for this. You don't know what to do with this phat-ass American pussy," Ceazia said playfully.

"Cha." Badman kissed his teeth.

He walked over and pulled her closer to him. She started walking backwards to get some space between them. Badman kept closing in on her. Eventually she ended up in the corner of the bedroom where she couldn't move anymore. Now that he had her cornered, Badman reached for her lips. Ceazia turned her head.

"Don't fight it, C. Me want you," Badman said, ripping the body piece right off of her.

His hands gently went from her ass to her breasts and then to her midsection. Her vagina was drenched in wetness. Again, Badman reached for Ceazia's lips and she couldn't hold out any longer. His tongue found its way to her nipples while his finger found its way to her clitoris. She looked up at the ceiling, wanting this moment to last forever. Her pussy quivered at the simple sound of Badman unzipping his jeans. After unbuttoning them and unbuckling his belt, his jeans effortlessly fell around his ankles.

"Stop," Ceazia hissed.

Badman ignored her comment while lifting her up and straddling her against the wall. He quickly threw on a condom and stuck his dick in her vagina.

"Ah fuck," Ceazia yelled as he pressed his manhood into her tight pussy.

"Me love a tight poom-poom," Badman said, making sure she felt every stroke over and over again.

"Oh shit. What are you doing to me?" Ceazia thought she was going to faint from pure satisfaction.

"This is true Jamaican lovemaking. Do you like it?" Badman asked between strokes.

Ceazia wouldn't answer because she didn't want to tell him the truth. His sex was the best she'd ever had. She couldn't answer because she was so overwhelmed with his dick. Badman started sucking on her left breast and literally pounded her against the wall. No longer able to fight it, Ceazia came all over his dick and the only word she managed to get out was his name, "Badman."

"Me a make you cum again and again." Badman carried Ceazia to the bed and turned her over. "Dis may hurt a little but you will like it." He repeated the same words he'd said to Danielle then he proceeded to position her just as he'd done with Danielle.

Just as Danielle had done, Ceazia assumed the position and got into an all-fours pose. "Take it slow," she whispered as she arched her back and pulled one butt cheek open.

"Damn," Badman said, thrown off by Ceazia's experience.

"Spit in my ass, baby," she begged for lubrication.

Badman spat as she requested then began to press the head of his penis in her ass. Ceazia dug her hands into the sheets and buried her face into the pillow as the head of his penis pressed against her anus. She closed her eyes and tried not to tense up. She knew within moments her ass would be just as wet as her pussy and it would be nothing but pleasure. After Badman got his penis in, Ceazia started massaging her clitoris, making the sex even more intense. Moments later the both of them released, and through it all, Ceazia's red stilettos never came off her feet.

Now satisfied sexually, it was time for Badman to put an end to the pleasure and handle fucking business. Like déjà vu, he began to tell his story to Ceazia about his work and how he was robbed and owed money, but this time he told it a little differently.

"You know me spend much time traveling from Jamaica to Florida. But me had to make a trip to Virginia. Dat dere was the first time me visit Virginia. Me use to do a lot of business dere but a while ago someone rob me for me money. Me wait and wait to get me money but it never came so me figure me better get it me self. So me ask around to find out what a really go on. Me hear about a dutty wicked gal dat rob man for dem money den kill dem."

Ceazia's heart raced and her stomach began to get that same sick feeling that Danielle had felt when Badman had told the story to her. Ceazia sat on the bed and hung onto every one of Badman's words.

"So when me find out dis here wicked, wicked gal rob the man of me money, me get vexed. So vexed me had to handle she personally."

Suddenly, Ceazia knew exactly what Badman was insinuating, but this is how she would prove to be different from Danielle. See, Ceazia went right into gangster mode. No tears ever welled up in her eyes as she began to put two and two together. She looked to her left in search for the gun that Badman had placed on the nightstand each night before they went to sleep. Noticing that it was still there, by instinct, she reached for it.

"You not want to do that," Badman noticed Ceazia's eye motion and grabbed her hand just as quick as she reached out. "All me want is me money. Just go to sleep. When morning come me a make you get the money and come," Badman said calmly.

Ceazia didn't say a word. She just looked at him in the eye. Her facial expression said it all. Badman had just written his death sentence. The last thing she could do was sleep. She had to figure out how she was gonna get out of this one. One thing she knew for sure was that she was not trying to come off her loot. She couldn't understand how one person's luck could be so fucked up. It was like she'd been cursed and would never shake it. There was no way Ceazia was going down like this; she refused. She didn't know how and when she was going to come out of this, but she vowed she would. After hours of constant tossing and turning, Ceazia finally fell asleep with Badman staring over her.

The next morning she awoke in bed alone. She sat up and listened for Badman. She heard the shower going and assumed he must be in the bathroom. She searched the room frantically, hoping to find his gun or anything that she could use a weapon.

"Jackpot," she whispered as her hand ran across the hard steel beneath the mattress.

Ceazia positioned herself on the bed so that she was sitting directly in front of the bathroom door. Breathing hard, she held the gun steady, pointing directly towards the bathroom exit. Ceazia's nerves began to get the best of her as she heard Badman turn the water off. For a split second she'd thought about shooting through the door. Feeling she was about to panic, she began pacing her breathing in an attempt to maintain her poise. She tightened her grip on the gun as the bathroom door crept open. Badman stood calmly as he stared death in the face.

"Do it. Me not tink you want to do that. You can't kill a Badman," Badman said, hoping his words would intimidate Ceazia and possibly save his life.

He'd totally forgotten about the gun under the mattress. It had been there since his last visit to Jamaica months ago. He cut his eyes to the left and glanced at the gun that he'd brought into the restroom that now rested on the top of the toilet tank. Knowing it was do or die he reached for it.

Boom, boom, boom. Motivated instead of intimidated by his words, Ceazia didn't waste another minute and pulled the trigger.

The shots sounded like that of a cannon. All three shots hit Badman, forcing him back into the bathroom and landing in the bathtub. Ceazia's hands shook uncontrollably as she crawled off the bed and walked into the bathroom.

"Oh God," she said before running out of the bathroom and vomiting all over the bedroom floor. "I've lost my touch," Ceazia said laughing, as she cleaned herself up.

She'd hit Badman in the chest, in the throat, and the final shot was to the dome. Frenzied, she grabbed all of her belongings and began to walk. Ceazia knew at the end of the road would be a busy street where she could get a cab. Although wandering alone on the island went against everything Badman had told her and she knew the odds of never making it out alive, she figured she'd just have to take her chances. With the gun still by her side Ceazia knew worse-case scenario she would have to kill again. Weary from the events and carrying her bags for such a long walk, Ceazia thought she would never make it to the end of the road. She knew she had to lighten her load. On her route she ran into a young girl.

"Excuse me," Ceazia called out. The girl stopped to see what the stranger wanted. "Here. You can have this if you like." Ceazia handed her one of her bags filled with clothes.

The girl reluctantly grabbed the bag then opened it to examine its contents. Seeing that it was a bag of beautiful clothes she was very excited.

"Tank you, tank you," she said as she rushed away.

Ceazia did not want to leave any evidence behind, but she was confident that the girl and those clothes would be long gone by the time the police arrived, if they ever did. Now that her load was much lighter, Ceazia could move a little faster. It took no time for her to reach her destination. Finally, at the busy road, she waited at the gas station. The first taxi she saw she asked for a ride. Immediately the taximan refused, stating that the travel from Ocho Rios to Montego Bay was too far. Moments later a resort van pulled up. As the driver got out and headed to the store she asked him for a ride to the Montego Bay Airport. Luckily, that was exactly where he was headed so he agreed. Ceazia tossed the gun in the large trash pile behind the building and hopped in the van. Although it was hot and uncomfortable, she was safe and that was most important. She rested her head back on the seat and relaxed, as she headed for home sweet home, but not really certain of just how sweet home would be by the time she got there.

Chapter 9

Ceazia nearly kissed the pavement when the plane landed and hit U.S. soil. Excited to be home, yet paranoid as hell, she called the only one that she could truly rely on, Diamond. She knew she had to get the fuck out of town and fast. Ceazia figured this would be the perfect opportunity to take Diamond on a little trip and show her how things should really be done. She finally had the opportunity to outshine Shawn and she planned to do it in a major way.

"Diamond," Ceazia said as soon as Diamond picked up the phone.

"What's up, baby? Where the hell you been? I was about to send out a damn missing persons report!" Diamond yelled.

"We're going to New York. Pack a few things. I'm on my

way home now. We'll talk about where I've been later," Ceazia instructed.

"Huh?" Diamond asked, baffled by this sudden trip, especially since she and Ceazia hadn't been on the best of terms and she'd been MIA for almost a week.

"We're going to New York. I'm booking our flight now," Ceazia reiterated.

Diamond spent no more time inquiring. After hanging up with Ceazia, she headed straight to the bedroom and began to gather her things. She called Shawn during the process.

"What's up, baby?" Shawn answered.

"New York," Diamond answered.

"New York?"

"Yeah. I'm going to New York."

"That's cool. That's my stomping grounds. What part?" Shawn inquired.

"I don't even know."

"Well, who you going with?" Shawn asked question after question.

"Ceazia. Who else?"

"That figures. Let me guess, she's trying to show you a better time than we had." Shawn knew exactly what to expect from Ceazia.

"I don't think so. She just decided to go to New York out of the blue," Diamond said, naive to the fact.

"All I can say is, be careful. For Ceazia to just get up and leave like that, she's got to have something up her sleeve. I know this girl and whenever she makes a quick move, it's for a reason," Shawn schooled Diamond.

"I'm sure I'll be okay. I've gotta finish packing. I'll be in touch." Diamond ended the call and proceeded to finish up her packing.

A little while later Ceazia came through the door and entered the bedroom. "You finish packing?" she asked, startling Diamond.

Diamond rushed over and embraced Ceazia. She hugged and kissed her intensely. Although she wasn't so sure about Ceazia at times, the thought of something happening to her tugged her heart. Ceazia showed just as much affection to Diamond in return.

"I'm almost done." Diamond turned her attention back on packing and threw a final few toiletries in her bag.

"Well, we need to hurry. The flight leaves in two and a half hours. We need to get to the airport." Ceazia grabbed the biggest piece of luggage she could find and threw in a few necessity items. Diamond looked at her in a peculiar way. "You'll thank me later," Ceazia replied as she grabbed Diamond's duffel and stuffed it in her oversized pilot bag. She'd hoped to do so much shopping that the now-empty bag would be filled with items they'd purchased during their trip.

"Let's roll," Diamond said as she grabbed her purse and keys.

They went through the house and checked all windows and doors to be sure they were locked and then they hit the road.

They arrived at the airport just in time. The line for the Delta flight going to La Guardia Airport was ridiculous. Five minutes later and they may not have been able to check their bags. After check-in they rushed through security to catch their plane. They arrived just as the plane was boarding. It was a full flight, but they sat comfortably in first class.

"Take note, baby," Ceazia grabbed Diamond's hand and whispered in her ear.

"What do you mean?"

"This is going to be a real trip. Take note of how I do things compared to how that broke-down Shawn did things. You were impressed by that shit because you knew no better. So I take that as my fault. Now I'm going to show you. So the next nigga will really have to step their game up," Ceazia said proudly.

"Oh, okay. So that's what this is about? You want to outdo Shawn?" Diamond said, realizing that Shawn was right.

"Nah, not totally. I want to show you a good time. We haven't really done any real shit lately." Ceazia covered things up, avoiding her true motive.

"Okay," Diamond said, disgusted by Ceazia's demeanor.

"Would you like a drink?" Their conversation was interrupted by the flight attendant.

"Yes, two white Zinfandels please." Ceazia ordered for the both of them then turned to Diamond. "This is just for now. You know when we go out it's nothing but the best. We popping bottles, baby."

Diamond didn't respond, she just rolled her eyes and began to look out the window. The more Ceazia talked the more she turned Diamond off. She was beginning to think everything Shawn said to her about Ceazia was true. Each day Ceazia would do something to prove Shawn right. Diamond had promised not to judge Ceazia based on someone else's feeling, but now Ceazia was doing a damn good job of showing her true colors.

To avoid any further conversation, Diamond put on her headphones and listened to some music. Forty-five minutes later they were in New York. They went from the baggage claim to Manhattan in a rush like the city was leaving in a few minutes. It was like Ceazia was so amped to show off that she was counting every minute. After checking into the W Hotel, Ceazia started planning.

"We'll go eat at Sushi Samba first. Then we can go by Sue's Rendezvous so you can see some real strippers and a real strip club."

"I don't think the strip clubs get any realer than the A." Diamond had to stop Ceazia in her tracks on that one.

"I'm sure I can change your opinion on that," Ceazia said confidently.

"I'm tired, baby. Why don't we order room service and start our day tomorrow," Diamond suggested.

"What? You are tripping. Don't tell me you came all the way to New York to be lazy. You were 'bout it 'bout it when you were in DC with ol' boy. Now you got the opportunity to have some real fun and you tripping." Ceazia sucked her teeth.

"All right, all right. I don't want you to feel like I don't appreciate what you are doing. I'm sorry. Let's roll." Diamond stood to her feet and followed Ceazia out the room.

They stood in front of the hotel as the bellman flagged a Yellow Cab for them.

"Oh my God," Diamond said, full of excitement as she noticed a few celebrities enter the hotel.

"That's right baby, you hanging with the stars." That boosted Ceazia's ego by one hundred points. Any other time she would have been trying to get at one of the celebrities, but since she was trying to be so Hollywood her damn self, she had too much pride. You would have never known she was nearly broke less than a week ago and near death less than twenty-four hours ago. Feeling on top of the world and like she was invincible, Ceazia put that whole Jamaica deal behind her and brushed her shoulders off.

"We're headed to Seventh Avenue and Barrow Street in the Village," Ceazia told the cabdriver like she was a native New Yorker as they hopped into the cab.

Twenty-five minutes later they arrived at the brightly-lit restaurant surrounded by colors of red and orange glass. After a nice dinner filled with spicy shrimp tempura and Pacific rolls and a seven-course *omakase,* and a number of Sake shots it was time to party. It was too early to head out for the club, but just in time for the strip club. So they headed to Sue's Rendezvous. Diamond compared everything from the building, the girls, and the patrons to the strip clubs she was used to back in Atlanta. Just like Magic City on a Monday, the club was packed. The only difference was it was Tuesday. The club was filled with patrons that included men, celebrities and ballers alike; and women bisexual, lipstick lesbian and butches alike. Those aspects didn't differ much from the clubs Diamond was used to. So she wasn't impressed. Next she began to look at the girls and the club setup. Now this is where she saw the difference. All the women seem to be from some sort of Spanish decent: Dominicans, Panamanians, Puerto Ricans, you name it. The club was set up like most clubs with a stage and pole, but the main stage was in the center of the bar and they also had girls dancing in cages. It wasn't the up close and personal one-on-one action that Diamond was used to in the A. Plus these chicks only danced topless and there were no table dances on the main floor. But like most clubs they had an area for private dances and that was the same no matter where you went. We all know what goes down in the champagne room!

Ceazia found a spot at the bar near the stage. As soon as they sat down a waitress was at their service. Ceazia wasted no time ordering a bottle of Rosé.

"I told you the white Zinfandel was only for the moment," Ceazia told Diamond after throwing her arm around Diamond's neck and pulling her close. She then gave her a wet kiss on the cheek.

"Here you are, ladies." As quick as the waitress left she had returned. She sat down the bottle of Rosé and two champagne glasses with it. "Will you all be sitting here or VIP?" she asked.

"We're good here for now, baby," Ceazia responded.

"Okay. Will there be anything else?" the waitress asked.

"Yes, can I get five hundred ones?" Ceazia gave her five one-hundred dollar bills.

"Baby, what are you doing?" Diamond looked at her like she was crazy as the waitress gathered the five one-hundred dollar stacks of one-dollar bills.

"We're enjoying ourselves." Ceazia blew her off, and then accepted the ones from the waitress.

"This is crazy. We haven't even been in the city four hours and you've already spent at least two thousand dollars," Diamond estimated, calculating the hotel, flight, dinner, and the money Ceazia was spending at the strip club.

"We're just getting started, baby. I'm gonna show you what it's really like to be balling." Ceazia was cockier than ever.

"Ceazia, please. You don't have to do this to compete with Shawn," Diamond pleaded.

"There is no competition, baby girl." Ceazia turned her attention to a dancer that walked by. "Yo . . . baby . . ." she called out to her.

"What's up, sexy," the dancer responded right away.

"Give my girl a private dance." Ceazia pointed to Diamond.

"Oh no, thank you," Diamond responded right away.

"Take the dance, Diamond," Ceazia insisted.

"C, please," Diamond continued to plea.

"You're insulting me. Now take the fucking dance, Diamond." Ceazia had spoken her final word.

Feeling like Ike and Tina and afraid that the next thing that Ceazia may say was, "Eat the cake, Ida Mae. Eat the fucking cake, Ida Mae," Diamond figured the safest thing to do was just to accept the dance.

Ceazia grabbed their bottle and they all went to the champagne room. Once situated the young lady began to dance. She didn't provide much entertainment as she swung her hair and swayed her body back and forth. One thing for sure was that this chick was no comparison to a private dance back in the A.

"What the fuck is this?" Ceazia said, noticing the lack of amusement.

"Excuse me?" the dancer snapped back.

"I mean you ain't doing shit. I'm paying you to dance, so dance, bitch," Ceazia snapped.

"I'm good." Diamond gave the young lady a twenty-dollar tip and told her she was free to go. She then directed her attention to Ceazia. "I don't know what your problem is, but you are really upsetting me."

"Oh, you're upset? You got balls now? So what? You call yourself snapping on me?" Ceazia noticed the firmness in Diamond's tone.

"You are seriously tripping. Please take me back to the hotel," Diamond requested.

"The W Hotel, fifteen-sixty-seven Broadway at Forty-Seventh Street, Times Square. Catch a cab." Ceazia pulled out two one-hundred dollar bills and sent Diamond on her way. She was going to ball out of control even if she had to do it by herself.

Diamond was appalled. She'd never seen Ceazia in this form. Unsure of whether she wanted to cry or cuss, she just grabbed her things and rushed out of the club. She flagged a cab and told the driver to take her exactly to the address where Ceazia had told her the hotel was at. The driver took her straight to her hotel. When she got safe to her room she finally had the courage to let her feelings go. Diamond sobbed uncontrollably as she thought about how terrible Ceazia had treated her. They'd never had so many problems as they had within the past few weeks. She could remember a time when they never disagreed, let alone argued. Diamond didn't even bother to call Ceazia and let her know she'd arrived safely. Hell, Ceazia hadn't called her. There was only one person on Diamond's mind and that's who she called.

"What's up, Lady Di," Shawn said through the phone receiver after seeing Diamond's number on his cell phone's caller ID. He was happy to see her name on his phone.

"I'm so hurt, baby. Ceazia has turned into a monster. I don't know what is wrong with her," Diamond explained.

"Baby, I've told you how Ceazia gets down. Now you're

seeing the true C. She could only hide it for so long," Shawn responded.

Diamond continued to tell Shawn all about their night from the time they got on the plane until the time she left the strip club. After an hour of talking and much support, Diamond advised Shawn she was going to take a shower and try to relax, then she got off the phone. She grabbed Ceazia's oversized bag and searched for her duffel. Diamond pushed aside a few of Ceazia's items then tugged on her duffel to get it out. As she pulled out her duffel a small Gucci knapsack popped out. Curious to see what was in it, Diamond opened the bag. To her surprise it was filled with money. She dumped it on the bed. She counted twenty thousand dollars.

"What the fuck did she do?" Diamond was frantic as all sorts of thoughts ran through her mind of how Ceazia could have come across that money.

Diamond didn't know if she should call Ceazia or Shawn. She figured she should confront Ceazia first so she called her cell.

"Yo," Ceazia yelled on top of the music that blasted in the background, indicating she was still at the strip club.

"Where did this money come from, C?" Diamond asked firmly.

"Hold on." Ceazia went to the bathroom so that she could hear a little better. "What did you say?"

"Where did you get all this money from?" Diamond asked again.

"Why are you digging through my stuff?" Ceazia answered her question with a question.

"Did you forget that you put my duffel inside your bag?

When I pulled my bag out, the knapsack came out with it. It was obvious there wasn't a pair of Gucci shoes in there so I peeped to see what it was," Diamond explained.

"Yeah, I'm sure, Diamond," Ceazia said, indicating she didn't believe her story.

"Could you please just answer my question?"

"Look, I came across a little basketball dude. We had sex and I'm sort of blackmailing him. Let's just call it my little version of a ghetto Kobe Bryant conspiracy." Ceazia laughed.

"So how much money did you get?"

"Fifty," Ceazia said reluctantly.

"Fifty thousand dollars!" Diamond exclaimed in astonishment. "Ceazia, this is serious!"

"You're right. That's some serious dough. And that's what I do; get money!" Ceazia hung the phone up in Diamond's ear.

Diamond just shook her head in disbelief as she headed to the bathroom. She started a steaming shower and hopped in. She stood beneath the hot water as all the stresses from her make-believe vacation washed away. Feeling a little better, Diamond decided to get out of the shower and put on her pajamas. Now relaxed, Diamond decided to call Shawn and update him on the drama. She knew Ceazia wouldn't be happy to know that she told Shawn everything that went on between them, but at this point she just didn't give a goddamn.

"Hey baby," Shawn answered right away.

"Hey."

"You feel a little better?" Shawn asked, knowing Diamond's intention to take a hot shower.

"Yeah, a little, but now there's even more to my drama here in New York. After I hung up with you I found a knapsack in Ceazia's bag with lots and lots of cash in it."

"What? How much?" Shawn inquired for his own personal reasons.

"Twenty thousand dollars."

"Did you ask her where it came from?" Shawn was excited that this may be the moment he'd been waiting for.

"Yeah. She claims she pulled a Kobe Bryant scandal on some basketball player and he paid her fifty grand to keep shit quiet."

"That shit don't surprise me. I told you she was about the dollar and would do anything to get it. Now you see?" Shawn knew deep in his heart there was more to the story and he was on a mission to find out.

"You're right. The more things come to the light, the more I feel like I don't even know Ceazia. At times I find myself thinking about how things would be without her. I mean, I'm seriously thinking about leaving her, Shawn." Diamond poured out her heart.

"Well, you know I'm gonna be biased to that, so I can't even give you my opinion, baby girl. All I can say is just go with your heart," Shawn said honestly.

"All right. Well, I'm gonna turn it in for the night. I'll call you tomorrow." Diamond hung up.

She pulled the covers back on the bed and grabbed the remote before getting comfortable in the bed. She flipped through channel after channel. Then she turned the television off completely and tossed and turned in an attempt to get comfortable. No matter what, she couldn't sleep. Something was missing. Diamond sat up and thought to herself. She knew she couldn't possibly be tripping over Ceazia like that. She thought about things a little longer and then it hit her; she needed a blunt. The whole day had gone by and she only had her morning dose. No wonder she was on edge all day. She figured maybe if she had her daily dosage of weed she would have been able to tolerate Ceazia a little more. Then she came to her senses. She realized it would not have mattered if she was on horse tranquilizers, she still wouldn't have been able to stomach Ceazia's brand-new attitude.

Since she had no weed to smoke, Diamond opened the bar and drank the miniature bottle of Belvedere. She took it straight to the head. Since she wasn't a regular liquor drinker, that Belvedere put her exactly where she needed to be. Now absolutely relaxed, she grabbed the remote and slid back beneath the covers. She flipped through the channels with nothing to watch, so she decided to glance through the movies the hotel had to offer. Finding just the right adult flick, she ordered right away. There was nothing like a good nut to top the night off and put her to sleep. She pulled her pajamas off and assumed the position to give herself pleasure. Just when she was ready to get started, in came the beast.

"What the fuck is going on in here? What? You got Shawn on speaker again?" Ceazia grabbed Diamond's phone. Diamond looked at Ceazia in disgust and rolled her eyes. "You don't need this shit." Ceazia turned off the porno. "I'm here now." Her words slurred as she took her clothes off.

Diamond could smell the alcohol on Ceazia's breath. She knew she was fucked-up. Diamond flinched and her body tightened as Ceazia touched her. As horny as she was before, she was totally turned off now. For the first time she was not attracted to Ceazia. She didn't want her in any way, form, or fashion.

"Relax baby, relax," Ceazia said with a mouthful of breast.

Diamond took a deep breath as Ceazia slid her hand between her legs.

"Damn, you not even gon' get wet for me?" Ceazia said, noticing the dryness of Diamond's midsection. "Don't worry. I got chu." Ceazia then disappeared beneath the covers.

She separated Diamond's legs and buried her head in her lap. Wanting this moment to be over, Diamond closed her eyes and relaxed. She pictured Shawn between her legs. She began to move her pelvis as she grabbed Ceazia by the hair.

"Suck this pussy," Diamond whispered as Ceazia's tongue went deep inside her. "Ah," she moaned with pleasure as she reached her peak. "Suck it, Shawn, suck it." Those words interrupted their sex like a scratched record at a party.

"What the fuck you say?" Ceazia threw the covers off the bed as she rose up.

"I'm sorry. I'm sorry, baby." Diamond immediately begged for forgiveness.

"Bitch!" Ceazia slapped Diamond in the face, surprising them both.

They both sat motionless, staring at each other in silence. Neither of them knew what to say or do. Diamond rolled over and buried her head in the pillow and began to cry. Ceazia threw on her clothes, grabbed her purse and the room key, and then headed out the door. As bad as Diamond wanted to call Shawn, she couldn't bring herself to do it. There was nothing Shawn could do. She'd gotten in this situation herself and she would have to get out alone. The only question was, how?

Chapter 10

The more Shawn thought about the sudden money Ceazia had come upon and the things Diamond had shared with him, the more he knew there was more to the story than Ceazia just schemin' some NBA star to keep quiet about their little rendezvous. He couldn't rest until he figured it out. Although Shawn was practically living out of a hotel and hadn't been home in several days or talked to Danielle just as long, he figured he'd see what was up with her. Hell, he had to start his detective work someplace; why not start at home?

When Shawn got home, he unlocked the door and headed inside. The house was quiet and Danielle was nowhere in sight. Actually, it looked as though no one had been there since the last time they were there together. Shawn found that strange. Sure, he knew Danielle was seeing someone, but it wasn't like her to just be ghost like that. He worried that maybe she had gone to the hospital to have her baby or something. Shawn called Danielle's cell phone, truly anticipating hearing her voice.

"You have reached—" the recording started to say before Shawn pressed the pound sign to bypass the recording and go straight to the beep so that he could leave her a voice message.

"This voice mail box is full," the recording informed him, so he disconnected the call.

It was at that point Shawn got a sick feeling in his stomach. That was definitely not like Danielle. All sorts of things began to run through his mind.

What if she's sick or locked up? What if she's hurt? What if the baby's hurt?

Thinking of the fact that Danielle was six months pregnant and nearly defenseless added even more paranoia to the situation. Shawn grabbed the house phone, intending to press *redial* to see the last number dialed, but as he hit the *talk* button the break in the dial tone notified him there were voice messages. He dialed the number to the voice mail box and entered the pass code immediately.

"You have twelve new messages, "the recording stated.

That sick feeling sunk in Shawn's stomach again. Too many negatives were appearing at one time. It wasn't like Danielle to play a disappearing act. She never had her phone off and if so, she would still check her messages. And just as she was persistent about her cell phone, she was the same way about the house phone. Shawn pressed the number one to retrieve the messages.

"Danielle, please call me when you get this message to let me know you are okay. I received a call from a young lady demanding fifty thousand dollars or I would never see you or the birth of my unborn child. Please call me," Shawn heard a male voice in a frantic state. Shawn pressed seven to delete that message and went on to the next. It was the same male voice from the previous one.

"Danni, this is Richard. Please call me. I couldn't risk losing you so I've sent the money. I just need to hear your voice to know that you're okay. Please call me." Shawn went on to the next message.

"It's me again. I'm not going to stop calling until I know that you're okay." Each message after that was the same.

Then there was one saved message. Shawn retrieved that message and listened to it. "Yo, pussywool, dis here is da bigman, Badman! For me to call you, you must know shit is real. Me not call again. Dis here is me last call!"

Shawn sat in a chair in his bedroom and placed his head in his hands. His head was all fucked-up. He thought of all the mean things he'd said and done to Danielle and wished he could take it all back. Sure, she wasn't always his favorite person to be around, but one thing for sure is she didn't deserve to be caught up in this. He could feel a lump begin to swell up in his throat as all sorts of thoughts ran through his mind.

"Get the fuck up, nigga! Get yourself together," Shawn said to himself as he jumped up out the chair. "Now think, nigga, think." He continued to talk to himself.

He reviewed everything in his head. *Danielle is missing. Richard paid fifty thousand dollars to a female for her ransom. Ceazia has fifty thousand dollars that she collected from a ballplayer. It has to be that conniving ass Ceazia.*

As quick as Shawn had begun his detective work, it was almost over. He knew Ceazia's devious ass had to be behind Danielle's kidnapping, but there were still some key points missing. He knew this wasn't a signature Ceazia move. In fact, this was nothing like a scheme she would pull off. She'd never been the type to kidnap. She was a quick mover, in and out. Shawn was sure someone else was involved, but who? He thought about everyone, not leaving out one person, making each person a suspect. There was only one person he could think of and that was Judah. Judah had a motive. Shawn figured he would hold on to Danielle to get at him for the money he owed, but that still didn't explain how Ceazia got involved. That was the question that haunted him. Shawn was determined to get to the bottom of things. He paced the floor back and forth as he thought. He remembered seeing Ceazia and Diamond talking with Judah after the club. He was sure that was when they linked up.

"I be damn!" Shawn said out loud as shit finally came together in his brain. "And all along I thought I was playing this bitch. These hoes were plotting on me just as hard as I was plotting on them," he said aloud as he flopped back into the chair he sat in before.

Shawn was sure he had it all figured out. How he saw it, Ceazia and Diamond had shit planned out from the night he met them. That was probably the reason Ceazia was out to get at him that night. Judah needed Ceazia to get to Shawn. He knew nothing about him, no phone, no address, and had no idea where he hung out. Yet being a nigga, one thing he did know for sure is that the next nigga would be weak for pussy. But when things didn't go as planned and Shawn hooked up with Diamond instead of Ceazia, she had to let her in on the scheme. And the rest was history.

Shawn was sure Diamond ran game on him so hard, getting all the information she needed and relaying it back to Ceazia. From there it went to Judah. But a couple of other things puzzled Shawn. He couldn't figure out why Diamond would tell him all the things she did if she was working with Ceazia to set him up. Also, he didn't know how Ceazia ended up with the money and why no one had contacted him for money. The whole purpose of the kidnapping would have been to make him pay.

"That fucking sneaky, grimy, scheming bitch." Shawn shook his head as he laughed. "She's done it again," Shawn said to himself, realizing Ceazia had come out on top once again.

Shawn realized exactly what had just happened. Ceazia had a plan of her own the whole time. That just goes to show you can never make a deal with the devil. He was sure when she made the arrangement with Judah her only role was to get the information so the kidnapping could take place. And probably after they collected the money from him they would hit her off with a small percentage. But Ceazia had a better idea. Instead of waiting for her cut, she called the one nigga she knew would pay up and got her money off the buck. With Diamond as her informant she already knew there was nothing jumping with Shawn and Danielle's relationship so the chances of getting him to pay was slim to none. Meanwhile, niggas was stuck trying to get at him to collect.

The more Shawn thought about the situation, the angrier he got. He cocked back his gun and released the bullet from the head as he thought about his next move. He knew it wouldn't be long before niggas were after him, but before he did anything he had one thing that was really eating him up inside and he wasn't quite sure how to handle it. Shawn couldn't believe Diamond had run game on him. His first instinct was to call Diamond and let her have it. Then he considered snatching her up and giving her a taste of her own medicine. All sorts of ideas ran through his brain as he took each bullet from his clip and wiped them with a polishing cloth, then reloaded it.

"Let's just think this shit through, homeboy," Shawn told himself, noticing the rage flowing through his body might be causing him to think erratically.

The last thing he wanted to do was react out of emotion. He had to sit and sort things out. There were too many unanswered questions. He asked himself question after question. *Would Diamond really set me up?* He thought of all possibilities. *Damn, my heart is telling me no, but then I know that bitch Ceazia got her brainwashed and she would do anything for her. But her feelings for me did seem so real when we were in DC. Fuck this; there is only one way to find out. I'm gonna tell that bitch the truth about everything.*

Shawn was going to tell Diamond everything from the original plan he and Danielle had to use Diamond to get at Ceazia, to his version about the kidnapping. Then depending on how that went, he'd plan to confess his true feelings to Diamond and try to make things work for them. Shawn took a deep breath as he picked up the phone to call.

"Where you at?" Shawn asked as soon as Diamond picked up the phone.

"The airport. What's wrong?" Diamond asked, sensing the frustration in his voice.

"Which airport?"

"Norfolk International Airport. Why? What is wrong,

Shawn?" Danielle asked again as she and Ceazia headed toward the baggage claim.

"We need to talk. I'll meet you at your house." Shawn hung up the phone.

He figured he would have more of an impact and be able to read her better if they spoke face-to-face. Shawn wasted no time jumping into his car and rushing to Diamond's home. He pulled up just as she and Ceazia were unloading their bags from the truck.

"I got it." Shawn grabbed Diamond's bag and totally ignored Ceazia.

He followed them into the house, placing Diamond's bags at the door of their bedroom.

"Okay, let's talk," Diamond said as she grabbed Shawn's hand and headed for the loft.

"This way." He pulled her through the front door and pointed towards his truck then led Diamond to the passenger side.

He didn't want to risk the chance of Ceazia hearing them talk. As soon as they both were comfortable in the truck he drove a few miles away to a secluded area. He didn't even want Ceazia in the immediate area. Besides, having Diamond far enough away would provide that extra bit of fear factor he needed to get the truth from her.

"I want to start by saying, I love you. You've changed my outlook on women. Because of you I no longer view women as bitches and hoes," Shawn started. "But I have to confess that I have not been totally honest with you. I'm going to say a lot of things and I just want you to hear me out." Shawn paused and took a deep breath before continuing. "From the time I met you, I had an ulterior motive. I was planning to use you to get at Ceazia. Danielle and I planned to set her up."

"What? What the fuck are you saying, Shawn?" Diamond interrupted Shawn, doing the exact opposite of what he'd asked.

"Please, hear me out," he continued. "Before I got locked up I used to provide Danielle's late boyfriend, Snake, with drugs. To make a long story short, Ceazia set him up and robbed him, but not before she killed him, his nephew, Duke, and her ex-boyfriend, Bear. That's why she fled to Atlanta." Shawn told the story as he knew it. "Needless to say, that set me back. But being a veteran in the game, it was nothing for me to make arrangements to pay the big man and still do a little something on the side. But when I went to jail it put me in a deeper hole. Danielle wanted to get even and I wanted my money; so we conspired to get Ceazia."

"This is just too much. I don't want to hear anymore. Please just take me home." Diamond began to cry. The truth was too much for her to handle.

"Sure, I'll take you home, but I think you should know where Ceazia really got that money from. She got it from Richard Anderson, Danielle's baby's father. And how was she able to get fifty thousand dollars from him? How about ransom? She conspired with the guys I owe to kidnap Danielle. And how did she get the information to do that? You. So what should I think about that? My first thought was to kidnap you and give you a taste of your own medicine. You conspired with Ceazia and used me to get Danielle. And to think the whole time you gave off this little naive, innocent vibe. I should have known you were

just like C's grimy ass. Birds of a feather flock together."
Shawn looked at Diamond for an explanation.

"I would never do a thing like that. I didn't know anything about that. Shawn, you've got to believe me. I care
about you, I really do. What can I do to prove it to you?"
Diamond pleaded, finally saying what Shawn longed to
hear.

"Tell me you will come with me. I've decided I no
longer want any parts of this shit. I just want to move back
to New York and start all over and I want you to come with
me," Shawn said sincerely knowing this would be the true
test.

"Okay. I will. Okay." Diamond said the words but wasn't
so sure if she meant them.

"Good. I just have a few loose ends to tie up, and in a
few days we can blow this joint." Shawn started the car and
drove Diamond back home.

He watched as Diamond walked in the house. He'd
told her the truth just to begin another lie. Yes, he loved
her and yes, he wanted to move back to New York, but not
before he got that fifty grand from Ceazia.

Chapter 11

The news of Ceazia's sudden winnings spread fast. This brought up a red flag with Judah. He of all people knew how she operated. He tried reaching Badman several times to tell him something was up but each time he called he had no luck. Hours later he received news that Badman was dead. Judah tried calling Ceazia and her number had been changed. Right away he knew she was a suspect. There was only one person he could use as a resource and that was Shawn. With that in mind he went to pay Danielle a little visit.

"Who is it?" Danielle said to the knock on her room door.

"Judah," he responded.

"Oh, now you come around. Where the hell is Pierre? This is ridiculous. I've been in this room nearly a whole fucking week," Danielle ranted.

"Badman is dead. Me tink C done da man and me need your help."

"No. This is just too much. I'm done with this," Danielle said, full of frustration.

"Whatever me get, me will give you half. Me not even want the money anymore. Me want she to suffer." Judah explained to Danielle that it was no longer about the money. It was strictly revenge at this point.

"Okay, I'll see what I can do. I just need to get home and get myself together. Give me a number I can reach you." Danielle grabbed a pen and paper.

"Here." Judah pulled out her phone and called himself then handed Danielle her phone.

"How'd you get this?" she asked, puzzled.

"Badman give it to me before him leave."

"Thanks. I'll be in touch." Danielle grabbed her things in a hurry and exited the room. She knew she was in some deep shit and would eventually need to get the hell out of Virginia, so she called her only true savior, Richard.

"Danielle, are you okay? How's the baby? Are you hurt?" Richard began asking questions as soon as he picked up the phone.

"What?" Danielle asked, confused.

"I got a call from some chick demanding fifty grand or I would never see the birth of my baby. I sent it to her a few of days ago but I still hadn't heard from you so I was worried," Richard explained.

"What? That shiesty little bitch! She thinks she's so fucking smart!" Danielle already knew what Ceazia had done. "Yes baby, I'm fine, but I need your help."

"You know this broad? What the fuck is going on, Danni?"

"It's a long story, baby, please, not right now," Danielle begged.

"Look, I'm arranging a chartered flight for you to come here. Once you're here we'll talk." Richard said. "I just need to get my baby out of harm's way."

"Okay, but give me a day or two to prepare," Danielle said, knowing she'd need to give Ceazia a little visit before her departure.

"Fine, but stay in touch. Have your phone on and answer when I call," Richard demanded.

"Okay," Danielle agreed.

"And Danni," Richard caught her before she hung up. "I love you."

Danielle's heart fluttered as the words registered in her brain. She couldn't remember the last time she'd heard those words, but damn, did it feel good to hear them again.

"I love you too, Richard. I never stopped." She disconnected the phone.

Fuming that Ceazia had pulled a fast one on her, Danielle was even more eager to settle the score. She called Ceazia's cell phone to only get a message from an operator that her number was no longer in service. With nowhere else to turn, she decided she would have to swallow her pride and look to Shawn for help. Danielle dialed his number and she was forwarded straight to voice mail. With no time to waste, she decided she'd have to get the information she needed on her own. She sped through traffic as she rushed home, praying that she wouldn't see Shawn. Once she got to their house and saw that it was clear and Shawn was nowhere in sight, she ran in and packed a few things then went and checked into another nearby hotel. Danielle didn't know what to expect or who she could trust so she was not taking a chance of going home and finding someone waiting for her. She'd seen the movie *Belly* several times and there was no way she was trying to take the chance of Chiquita falling from the ceiling and slicing her throat like a loaf of bread as she had done Lenox in the movie.

Once Danielle checked into the hotel, she immediately pulled out her laptop and connected to their wireless Internet. She pulled up Shawn's cell phone bill. She looked at the numbers he called most often and spent the most time talking. She came up with two numbers. She knew that one had to be a cell for Diamond and the other her house phone. By looking at the first three digits she was able to determine which was home and which was cell. Danielle started with home. She pressed *star 67* from her cell to block her number and dialed.

"Hello." Ceazia answered the phone with caution. Any other time she would have placed anonymous call block on her phone but until that moment no one ever called the house except for Diamond and Shawn and they had no reason to block their numbers.

"You thought you were so fucking smart, you little trifling bitch," Danielle spat. "You thought your plan was foolproof, didn't you. Well, it wasn't. I'm here and I want my fucking money. And I don't just want the fifty grand. I want one hundred; fifty you stole from my baby father and the fifty you stole from Snake. Meet me at Princess Anne Park tomorrow at noon. No bullshit." Danielle hung up without waiting for a response.

Ceazia had forced Danielle to be a totally different person. She'd brought out a part of her she had no idea existed. There was no denying her days as a gangster's girl had finally come in handy. For the sake of survival, she had to do the unthinkable and goddamnit she was willing. She was confident her plan would work and Ceazia would meet her at the park as arranged. One thing she knew for sure, there was no way Ceazia wanted to go back to jail.

Now that Danielle had taken care of the Ceazia portion of the plan, it was time to hold up her end of the bargain with Judah. She called him and told him her plans to meet Ceazia at the park the next day; but she conveniently left out the fact that she would be collecting fifty grand and that she would be setting Ceazia up to get arrested.

The next day came like nothing. While Danielle sat with the homicide detectives counting down the minutes to her meeting with Ceazia, Shawn was headed to Diamond's house.

"Hey baby." Diamond met him with a kiss at the door.

"What's up, sexy?" Shawn followed her into the house and up the stairs to the loft.

It didn't take a whole five minutes before Ceazia pranced her ass up the stairs. "You here again? You ain't got shit better to do?" she spat at Shawn.

"You ain't got shit better to do?" Shawn spat Ceazia's own inquiry right back to her.

"This is what I do; I regulate shit," Ceazia said with hands on hips.

It had become routine for Ceazia to antagonize Shawn at every visit.

"You guys, please. Do I have to go through this shit

every time you two are in the same damn room together?" Diamond begged them to stop as she prepped a blunt.

"Every day since we've come back from New York this nothing-ass nigga has been here," Ceazia snapped.

"Bitch, the only reason you still standing is out of respect for Lady Di," Shawn responded, knowing that the only reason he was there was to make sure Ceazia didn't do or say anything that may keep Diamond from coming with him to New York as planned.

"Bitch? Yeah, I got your bitch. And I mean that literally, muthafucker," Ceazia said before checking the time on her phone. "Matter of fact, the both of them. I'm 'bout to add the other to my list right now." Ceazia exited the loft and then headed out the door to go meet Danielle.

She searched through her phone to find the cell number she'd saved and gave Danielle a call on her way out but all she got was voice mail. She decided to leave her a message.

"You know I'm not the type to just trust you will hold up your end of the bargain. So I will be arriving empty-handed but I will give you the key to the treasure," Ceazia said, hoping that Danielle would get the picture that she would not be bringing the money with her but would let her know where she could get it. Plus, this gave her the opportunity to cheat. There was no way Ceazia was giving Danielle what she expected. For one, she didn't have it and if she did she still wouldn't come up off it. She set aside a small amount to give Danielle and placed a small IOU note with a smiley face drawn on it in the bag.

Shawn sat on the couch for a moment and thought about the words Ceazia had just said to him. He knew she had something to do with Danielle's kidnapping and that little comment had just confirmed it. He tried calling Danielle's phone and just as many times before it went straight to voice mail. Knowing that something was fishy, Shawn jumped up from the couch and grabbed his keys.

"I'll be back," he yelled to Diamond as he rushed out the door and jumped in his truck.

He caught up with Ceazia at the light around the corner. He slowed up as he proceeded cautiously to follow her. He knew Ceazia would constantly be in her rearview since she knew the ropes from her time in the game. But at the same time, Shawn was sure not to lose her because he knew she would lead him straight to Danielle.

Back at the precinct, Danielle waited patiently for her big moment; the moment she had been waiting for, when she would bring Ceazia Devereaux down once and for all.

"Are you ready?" Detective Tarson asked Danielle with irritation.

"Yes, we've gone over this for the past four hours. I got it," Danielle assured him, adjusting her earpiece.

The wire microphone was uncomfortable lying between her breasts. She began to think her plan wasn't such a good idea after all. She realized as the detectives briefed her over and over again that this was more than she'd anticipated. She'd been there since six-thirty in the morning. The chicken biscuit and bottle of water she had for breakfast had long been digested, plus her hunger for her money was ripping her stomach apart. Irritated and impatient, Danielle was more than ready to get this shit over with.

"I don't have to remind you that if you don't deliver,

your deal is a wrap. You're not too far away from a jail cell yourself for withholding information," the detective explained for the eighth time.

"I told you I got it," Danielle said sternly, looking right into his tired eyes.

"I've been working on this case far too long to let it become shit," Detective Tarson announced, pouring his fourth cup of coffee for the day.

"Not to mention, you're up for captain," Danielle added to let him know she was aware of his true motive.

"Where did you hear that?" he inquired.

"Detective, a word of advice, if you plan on holding a conversation with your comrades after you leave the interrogation room, then don't keep the door cracked open," Danielle explained.

"You shouldn't have been eavesdropping."

"Huh? You're one to talk. That's what you and these other stale-coffee drinkers and Krispy Kreme doughnut eaters do to earn a paycheck on the fifteenth and end of the month, right? Now, let's go so I can do this and never see your fat ass ever again," Danielle proclaimed, heading towards the door with her car keys in hand.

Paying no attention to the team of police behind her, Danielle thought about revenge her entire ride. *I couldn't even sleep last night anticipating this final encounter with Ceazia. That bitch wants it all and will rob, steal, and kill for it. In turn, she's going to be getting a lovely 10 x 4 jail cell.*

On the way over to the park, it was like Danielle caught every red light on her route. Her hands clenched the steering wheel. She couldn't stop thinking about all that money she would have and how she would spend it. As she pulled up near the park, she glanced in her rearview mirror one last time to be sure Detective Tarson and his clan were following her as planned. Sure enough, they were in hot pursuit in a cleaning van following close behind her. She knew Ceazia was unpredictable and wasn't scared to kill; therefore her safety totally depended on the protection of the officers.

Danielle was grateful she arrived at the park first. This gave her an opportunity to collect her thoughts. Before getting out the car she turned her cell phone on and checked her messages. She heard Ceazia's message. "That bitch has got something up her sleeve. Oh well, it is what it is," Danielle said, realizing it was too late to do anything about it. "I've just got to go with it for now," she said to herself, knowing Ceazia wasn't trustworthy. Danielle got out the car and found an empty bench that was facing the parking lot, giving her a full view of Detective Tarson and the cleaning van. She glanced around the park expecting to see Judah hiding someplace, but he was nowhere to be found. Three small children and their mother were playing on the swings nearby. She hoped that would deter Ceazia from doing anything too crazy. She also prayed she wouldn't say anything about the money. Looking up at the sky, Danielle whispered, "God, there has to be a better way to live," realizing she'd done all the wrong things to reach her goals in life.

Thirty minutes later and a stop in Tarson's never-ending gripes, Ceazia pulled up. She took her time getting out of the truck and then strolled over to Danielle.

"What's up?" As Ceazia shook Danielle's hand, a small envelope was given to her. Done like a drug dealer and fiend during a drug buy, there was no way Tarson and his team could have seen it.

"Showtime," Tarson whispered into the earpiece.

"Now why the beef, Danielle?" Ceazia asked with pure sarcasm.

"Bitch, don't play with me," Danielle responded, angered by Ceazia's sarcasm.

"Whatever, I see you truly think you're real gangster. You talked a lot of shit over the phone." Ceazia subtly let Danielle know she wasn't as nearly gangster as she tried to portray.

"In case you didn't know, I don't bluff," Danielle said, shaking her head and trying to stand her ground.

"I'm sure you know my history. Hell, that's why you're here. You see me, the person that stands before you; I am a true gangster's girl. Just being with the nigga doesn't mean you've earned the title. Unless you've grinded, schemed, sexed, and killed a nigga all in the name of drugs or for the love of money, then you have no idea what it's like to be a gangster's girl. After Vegas, I had to take what I could get. Yeah, I set Snake up, and Duke and Bear just happened to be in the wrong place at the wrong time, but all in all, those muthafuckas got what they deserved. I would hate for something to happen to you and your unborn child," Ceazia ranted as she looked Danielle up and down.

Sensing Ceazia's aggravation, Danielle toned it down a couple of notches. "Please, I'm not here to cross you. I just want to know the truth."

"Listen carefully, because I'm only going to say this once." Ceazia went on to tell Danielle all about Snake's death. "First I have to say none of that shit was planned to go down the way it did. It was as much as a surprise to me as it may be to you. I was forced to make the decision I made. It was simple. Snake and I had a little arrangement, so he thought. I was going to give him some much-needed information about his brother's death and he was going to pay me for it. Normally people separate business and pleasure, but for us it went hand in hand. So we decided to have a little rough sex, which was really good, if I may add." Danielle took a deep breath as the thought of Snake screwing Ceazia made her faint. Trying to keep her composure she listened calmly. "But to the both of our surprise my ex-boyfriend, Bear, ran in on us with gun in hand. Automatically my fight-or-flight instincts kicked in so I told him Snake was raping me. Then to make matters worse that little pussy-whipped Duke came running in deciding to ruin the party. Two's a party, three's company. He ran through the door busting shots and hit Bear once in the chest. Then I guess he began to think about how good I'd fucked him and he turned on Snake and told him to get on the ground." Danielle felt disgusted knowing that Ceazia had sexed both Snake and Duke. She listened on as Ceazia continued. "Seconds later there was another shot fired that hit Snake, then he shot two more as he fell to the ground that hit Duke and killed him." A huge lump formed in Danielle's throat as the events of that night unfolded. It took all she had to refrain from bursting into tears, but she listened on. "But the fucked-up shit about it was that shot that hit Snake wasn't from Duke, it was from Bear. Then with Snake still holding his gun I sent the final shot to Bear's head killing him. So you see I didn't kill anyone except Bear. Bear killed Snake and Snake killed Duke." Ceazia told the story with no emotion like it was nothing for her to be involved in a triple murder.

Fifteen minutes had passed and Danielle was in the

clear. She'd gotten Ceazia to confess so shit was a wrap. She was at a loss for words and she felt that she might burst into tears at any moment.

"Well, I've got to go," Danielle said the least, rising from the bench, wishing she could just run to her car and cry.

"Until next time." Ceazia smirked.

"Yeah, all right," Danielle added and proceeded to walk away.

She wanted to run to her car and bury her head. To finally hear how Snake was killed and to vision all the details really hurt her.

Confident that she'd come out on top, Ceazia walked away from the bench wearing a devious grin. A few steps into her victory trot Tarson and the other detectives moved in like a swarm of killer bees and Ceazia was their honey for the day.

"Get on the ground . . . put your hands up . . . don't move." The detectives shouted command after command as they rushed Ceazia, forcing her to the ground and handcuffing her. She put up no fight. Once the cuffs were secure Detective Tarson brought Ceazia to her feet. She and Danielle locked eyes as she was being escorted to the police car. A cold shiver ran through Danielle's body as she looked at Ceazia. It was like she could feel the defeat. This was probably the first time Ceazia had shown weakness and Danielle was the witness. She would never forget seeing the terror in her eyes.

In the car Danielle took a look at the mini-envelope. It read: *VB YMCA #12*

Inside the envelope was a small key. She thought for a moment before she realized what it was. "Virginia Beach

YMCA locker number twelve. And this is the key to my treasure," Danielle thought aloud. "Yes! YMCA, I'm on my way to collect my fucking winnings," she said, then sped out of the parking lot in a hurry figuring maybe this one time Ceazia actually kept her word.

Chapter 12

"Lead me to the pot of gold, my little leprechaun," Shawn said as he followed Danielle from Princess Anne Park.

He was glad to see that Danielle was okay but he wasn't too sure exactly what was going on. He wouldn't be surprised if she was trying to collect on the loot without him. At this point everyone was a suspect. Shawn drove close, sure not to lose her. He knew from Danielle's history that she wouldn't be monitoring her mirrors as she should. After ten minutes of traveling, he wondered where the hell they were headed. Moments later he followed her into the parking lot of the Virginia Beach YMCA.

"I know this bitch is not going to work out," Shawn said as he parked his car on the other side of the building, opposite from where Danielle had parked.

He got out of his car and followed her into the building. He watched her walk into the ladies' bathroom. Preparing to have to wait at least an hour if she did decide to work out, Shawn decided to go back to his truck and wait. Little did he know, someone else planned on waiting as well.

"Look at this stupid nigga. Him so focused on that bitch him not even know me a follow him," Judah said, watching Shawn from his parked car.

Judah was relieved when he saw Shawn at the park. He thought all hopes were dead when Ceazia was arrested, but Shawn fell right into his plot. Not really trusting anyone at this point, Judah felt like Shawn and Danielle might be trying to run a little game of their own. Judah entered the building and made his way toward the women's locker room prepared to snatch Danielle and find out what the fuck was going on. There he saw a disgusted Danielle exiting with a small sports bag. Making note that Danielle entered the center empty-handed and now she was exiting with a bag, Judah figured that could only mean one thing. That had to be a stash spot. But from the look on Danielle's face, she was not happy with its contents.

Judah had no idea what arrangement Ceazia and Danielle had made, and at this point he didn't care. But with Ceazia being the slickster of the two, he wasn't surprised that she didn't keep her end of the bargain. Judah refused to leave empty-handed, though, so whatever Danielle did have, he wanted it. And by all means he was going to get it. His hunger for the money was the only thing keeping Danielle alive; otherwise he'd kill her ass just at the slightest idea that she had involvement with the death of Pierre. Judah followed Danielle out of the YMCA and rushed back to his car. He watched Danielle pull out and then waited for Shawn to follow. Finally he pulled out, being the caboose to the train.

"I can't believe this shit! I knew I couldn't trust that bitch. Now what am I supposed to do?" Danielle said out loud, pissed that she'd only received ten thousand dollars.

Ceazia had shorted her ninety thousand dollars and there was no way she could just let it go. This was the last time she would allow Ceazia to get away with taking something from her. She'd robbed her of her man when she took Snake's life. She robbed her of her happiness and livelihood when she took Snake's money, leaving her to struggle. And now she'd robbed her baby's father. That was the last straw. Danielle refused to let things ride. She wanted her money and she wanted every penny. Having no one else to depend on but Shawn, Danielle called him.

"Hello." Surprisingly, Shawn not only answered, but answered on the first ring.

"Shawn, it's Danni. I believe Ceazia is sitting on a stack of money," she said, calculating the fifty grand she collected from Richard plus the fifty that she was suppose to pay her. She estimated at least one hundred grand. "She's in jail so now is the perfect time for us to make our move. All I need you to do is call Diamond and find out where Ceazia is keeping the stash," Danielle begged, unsure that Shawn was willing to cooperate.

"I'll try," he said with little emotion.

"Trying ain't enough. Damn, Shawn. Can you please do something? I've practically done everything to get this fucking money. In the beginning it was supposed to be us; but somehow it's turned out to be me. It's ninety thousand dollars, Shawn, ninety fucking thousand." Danielle began to cry hysterically.

"I'll see what I can do," Shawn said calmly, then disconnected the call.

Although Shawn agreed, he had plans of his own. With the information Danielle shared he knew exactly how to move. He exited off from Danielle. Now it was time to use Diamond to his advantage.

Noticing Shawn was no longer following Danielle, Judah exited in a different direction as well, choosing to follow Shawn. He wasn't sure what was up, but he just had to go with his gut on this one. He would keep a constant monitor on Shawn. He was sure that he was the one who would lead him to the money without a doubt.

"Hey baby," Shawn said into his phone receiver after calling Diamond right away.

"Hey Shawn, what's up?" Diamond replied.

"Remember how I told you I wanted us to move to New York and leave all this behind?" Shawn referred back to their previous conversation.

"Yes," Diamond said nervously as she wondered what was wrong.

"Okay, and you know how I said all this shit started behind Ceazia robbing me; leaving me owing some people."

"Yes," Diamond answered, still nervous.

"Well, I still owe them and I want to get this cleared up before we go. That fifty thousand dollars Ceazia has stashed away that she took from Danielle's baby father; do you think you can find out where it is?" Shawn asked uneasy because he wasn't sure how Diamond would react.

"I don't know, Shawn. Then I would be robbing her. I don't want to get involved in this."

"But baby, look at all she's done not only to you but so many other people. She's poison, Diamond. She needs a taste of her own venom." Shawn tried his best to convince her.

"Fine. I'll see what I can do," Diamond said reluctantly before hanging up the phone.

She thought about how she would ask Ceazia about the location of the money as she dialed her number.

"You have reached—" the automated voice began to say, indicating Ceazia's phone was off.

Knowing that was not like Ceazia to have her phone off, Diamond continued to call her phone a number of times. She figured maybe Ceazia was in a spot that she couldn't receive service. After thirty minutes of continuous voice mail, Diamond began to worry. Diamond looked at the time. It had been a couple of hours since her and Ceazia had last spoken. She could only hope that everything was okay, but her gut was telling her differently.

Chapter 13

"Jesus," Diamond jumped out of her sleep in the middle of a nightmare.

A wicked vision of Ceazia's dead body hanging from a man-made rope made from a bedsheet haunted her. She noticed the house phone was ringing off the hook once she came to.

"Hello," she rushed to answer.

"You have a collect call from," the automated voice recited, "C," Ceazia's voice filled in the blank.

Diamond wasted no time accepting the call. "C, what's going on?" she asked as soon as the call was connected.

"That bitch Danielle set me up. She's really on some shit, Diamond. Like this bitch thinks she's a true gangster and shit," Ceazia ranted on and on.

"Danielle? Since when do you deal with her?" Diamond

asked, hoping this would lead into the conversation she and Shawn previously had.

"It's a long story, Diamond." Ceazia tried avoiding the conversation.

"Umm, maybe you haven't noticed, but you're in jail, C. All you have is time," Diamond said sarcastically.

"Look, the night you and Shawn hooked up, Judah called me and asked that I help him get some money back that Shawn owed him. So I agreed." Ceazia told half the story.

"That still doesn't explain your dealings with Danielle or why you're in jail right now," Danielle said, wanting to get more detailed information from Ceazia.

"Okay, listen up because I'm only saying this once. Judah wanted me to find out any information I could about Shawn and Danielle. He wanted to arrange to have Danielle kidnapped so that Shawn would be forced to pay him his money by means of ransom. But knowing that Shawn wasn't feeling her like that, I knew it would be unlikely that he would pay. I needed a backup plan so I decided to collect from Danielle's baby father. The whole time Danielle had a plan of her own. She called me up and basically blackmailed me. She said I had to pay her one hundred grand or she would go to the police and tell them I killed Snake, Duke, and Bear. Needless to say, I arranged to give her the money, but that bitch still set me up and now I'm in here with no fucking bond!"

"So you paid her the one hundred grand?" Diamond hoped she was smarter than that.

"Hell nah! You should know better than that. I gave that bitch ten grand," Ceazia laughed.

"So where's the rest?" Diamond asked.

"There is no ninety grand. All I have is the fifty I got from her baby father and it's in a safe place."

Not wanting to press the money issue, Diamond moved on to another question she needed answered. So far things were just as Shawn had told her.

"So how'd you know all the information to tell Judah?" Diamond asked, knowing exactly what the answer was. She just wanted to hear Ceazia say it.

"I mean, some stuff was obvious," Ceazia said, not wanting to admit she'd used Diamond.

"So what about the stuff that wasn't so obvious?" Diamond forced Ceazia to answer her.

"Well, I guess some stuff I knew from you too," Ceazia admitted.

"I knew it. The entire time you were using me. That's why you encouraged me to talk to Shawn because you needed him to get to Danielle. You betrayed me, C," Diamond said, sincerely hurt.

"But baby, I did this for us. How else were we going to survive? If you haven't noticed, neither of us work. Where do you think the money was coming from? From the jump I told you we needed to get at Shawn for money purposes but you didn't have it in you to run game on him. After a while I saw that you were into him and I couldn't depend on you to run game so I had to take matters into my own hands." Ceazia just put it out there.

"C, it had to be a better way."

"Baby, I'm a hustler. For the past few years I've had to fight and grind to make ends meet so this is all I know. I couldn't have you here with me and let things fall apart. You depend on me to make sure ends meet so I had to do what I had to do." Ceazia turned things around like it was for Diamond that she'd done these things.

"I understand. I never looked at it that way," Diamond said submissively. "So what do we do to get you out of there?"

"I've got a lawyer, a real good one that works miracles. He's the only one I trust to handle my case." Ceazia proceeded to give her the name and number of the attorney.

"I got it. And just how am I supposed to pay him along with all the rest of the bills? Like you said, I don't have a job." Diamond was going to force Ceazia into telling her where the money was if it killed her.

"Diamond, you know you're all I have right now?"

"Yes, I do, Ceazia, and that goes both ways. You're all I have as well." Diamond was sure to tell Ceazia exactly what she wanted to hear.

"If there is anyone I can trust, it would be you. My whole life I've had people turn their back on me, leave me standing alone, and even stab me in the back. That had ruined the chance of anyone ever getting close to me again. But I still let you in. You've been nothing but loyal to me since day one. And I hope that never changes." Ceazia gave her speech, hoping to change any thought Diamond may have had about stealing the money.

"No need to say all of that, C. I got your back and you don't have to worry about me stealing from you."

Ceazia took a deep breath then carried on. "In the attic in a box labeled *kitchen* you'll find the duffel bag."

"Okay, I'll call your lawyer and get right on it. Don't worry, baby, I'm going to make sure everything is all right," Diamond assured Ceazia.

"You have thirty seconds remaining," the recording interrupted their call.

"I love you, Diamond. Please don't let me down," Ceazia said, knowing what could possibly be in store for her.

"Love you too." Diamond managed to squeeze in those last words before their call was disconnected.

Diamond wasted no time getting on the job. She contacted the lawyer then collected the cash. Concerned and scared, she began to pack for relocation herself. She made arrangements to live with some relatives in California, purchased her ticket, and rented a car to get to the airport. Since she wasn't sure what would happen next, she also sent herself a care package to meet her in California. Ceazia had really gotten herself involved in some deep shit and Diamond wasn't feeling that at all. She'd gone through enough drama in her younger days to last her a lifetime. Besides that, she didn't know if she could really trust Ceazia after all. It turned out everything Shawn said about her was true. Diamond figured if Ceazia was deceitful enough to use her for her own personal gain, then she was capable of doing any damn thing.

Chapter 14

"This is some bullshit!" Shawn slammed the phone down.

He'd spent the entire morning calling Diamond and he hadn't been able to reach her. He took turns calling her cell and the house. With no other alternative, he decided to pay her a visit. He had butterflies in his stomach. He didn't know if that was a warning that something was wrong or if it was a warning that Diamond was up to some sneaky shit. Whichever it was, he was gonna follow his instincts and go to her house. He continued to call her phone the entire way. Caught in the Downtown Tunnel traffic, Shawn dialed Diamond's numbers back-to-back; the house phone and the cell phone.

"Honk, honk!" a horn blew, startling him.

He looked up to moving traffic. Shawn pressed the gas

to catch up then glanced up to see exactly who the impatient bastard was that was rushing him.

"Oh shit," he said, noticing it was Judah. "Just my fucking luck!" Shawn didn't think Judah saw him, but sped up and tried to lose him just in case.

A few miles down the road Judah was no longer in sight. Shawn took his time exiting the interstate and heading into Diamond's neighborhood. He gave her phone a few more rings before turning on her street. His heart dropped to his balls as he pulled up.

"You going somewhere?" Shawn asked as Diamond packed a rental car full of bags.

"Umm . . . yeah, um, just for a few days," Diamond stuttered, obviously nervous.

"Oh yeah. Where you going?" Shawn inquired.

"Back to Atlanta," Diamond lied.

"That's a lot of bags. Need some help?" Shawn grabbed at the bag on Diamond's shoulder.

"I got it." Diamond pulled back.

"No you don't." Shawn pulled his gun out and put it to her waist. "Let go of the fucking bag and go back into the house." He snatched the bag from her hand and followed her into the house and to her bedroom.

"Sit," Shawn instructed as he opened the bag, revealing the money inside. "You just like that bitch you with." Shawn shook his head in disbelief.

"Shawn, please. I didn't know what to do," Diamond pleaded.

"I actually trusted your lying ass and you still fucked me like the rest. All y'all bitches the same. That bitch Ceazia robbed me and got away with it. Danielle robbed me and got away with it; but you know what? It won't happen a third time, bitch." Shawn grabbed Diamond by her hair, forcing her to her feet. "You ain't gone get away with it."

"Please baby, don't do this. We can still leave together."

"Oh yeah. You love me, huh? You want to be with me?" Shawn pushed Diamond against the wall and started feeling her up, squeezing her breasts and ass.

"Just take the money. Just take it and leave," Diamond begged, truly just wanting Shawn to take the money.

"Don't worry, I'm going to take the money but not before I take something else I want and fucking deserve." Shawn threw Diamond on the bed.

Diamond lay motionless as Shawn pulled off her clothes piece by piece. All he could think about was how tight her pussy would be when he forced his dick deep inside her. He unzipped his pants and pulled out his penis without even pulling his boxers down. He sucked her breasts and rubbed his fingers across her clit until he felt her wetness seep out, making his dick rock solid.

"You ready for this dick?" Shawn said as he pushed his raw penis inside her. "This is what it feels like to get fucked." He pounded and pounded Diamond as she lay on the bed, immobile. "Where you want this cum? You want it on those big-ass titties or should I just cum in this hot pussy? You know what I think, I'll bust in your lying mouth." Shawn pulled out just before he began to bust and put his dick in Diamond's face. "Drink this fucking cum, bitch," he said as he jerked his dick, forcing the cum out all over Diamond's face.

Shawn hopped up and pulled up his pants without even wiping his dick clean. He grabbed the bag and money and headed out the door.

"Shawn!" Diamond yelled out. Shawn looked over his shoulders to hear her final words. "Seeing happy children makes me smile. Thinking of my childhood makes me cry. I'm afraid of being alone . . . and my deepest secret is I was raped by my foster dad." Diamond answered the questions Shawn had asked her so many times before.

Although those words ripped through Shawn and made him want to vomit, he still kept his ice grill on as he walked out the front door and hopped into his truck. He had to make one quick stop by his crib and he was off to New York. He called Danielle to tie things up between them.

"What's up?" she answered.

"She ain't budging, yo. She claims she doesn't know nothing 'bout the money. Shit here too hot, you need to lay low. I'm leaving the scene for a while myself." Shawn said everything he could in hopes to scare Danielle back to Atlanta.

"Aight." Danielle didn't put up a fight. She was tired and ready to give up anyway.

"Gone." Shawn hung up.

Those last words Diamond said began to haunt Shawn as soon as he hung the phone up. Her words kept running through his head over and over again as he drove. She had him so fucked-up that he almost ran into the back of a car. Deep in throught the entire ride home, Shawn never even realized Judah was hot on his trail. Judah had followed him to Diamond's house and sat outside until he left. Then he continued to follow him home. He watched Shawn as he rushed in the house.

Wasting no time, Judah cocked his gun and rushed in behind him. Standing at the front door Judah started to kick it in, but something just told him to try the knob.

Fucking idiot ting dat, he thought as he quickly pushed the door open, ready to bust shots at the first thing moving. And that is exactly what he did when he saw Shawn dive onto the living room floor, attempting to hide behind the sofa. There was no hiding from those hot balls Judah was about to fire in his ass, though. This was a long-awaited moment and it felt like he was busting a nut as Judah fired shot after shot into Shawn's body. And like a nut, once it was over, it was no fun, so Judah grabbed his bag of goodies and headed straight to the airport. Now twenty grand richer and a settled score, Judah felt like he could finally return home to Jamaica and ease his mind.

Epilogue

The smell, sounds, and uniforms were all too familiar as Ceazia took her clothes off for a strip search and collected her jumpsuit and bedding. Jail was just not something she was trying to relive. Veteran to the game, she already knew the ropes. She was escorted to her cell and introduced to her cell mate, Sara. She reminded her a lot of her old cell mate, Brook, from the Virginia State Penitentiary for Women. She could only hope nothing else would be like the state pen. As Ceazia adjusted to her new environment she said little and observed a lot. She had a little rank because her name rang bells but just as many chicks wanted to test her. Her first few days were fine. She stood her ground and developed a little crew but when one particular person stepped on the scene shit came crumbling down and Ceazia's jail stay turned into a living hell.

"Identify yourself, inmate," a woman deputy yelled, sending paralyzing chills down Ceazia's spine.

Ceazia stood motionless as the familiar voice rang through her ears. Her stomach turned as she thought back to the days she'd had run-ins with this same deputy.

"Identify yourself, inmate," the deputy yelled again while tapping Ceazia on the shoulder with her baton.

"You know exactly who I am," Ceazia said, staring at the deputy face-to-face.

"Welcome to my world, bitch. You are now in hell and I am the fucking devil," The deputy said, walking away.

Ceazia knew what was in store and just like she'd said, she couldn't do another jail sentence. Just the fact that she was there nearly drove her insane, plus the added misery of that deputy was just too much. It was just like the jails people hear about on the streets and see on the damn news report shows. The grime was worse in the joint than on the streets. So when Ceazia found out how the deputy ran shit and all the shit that was going down on the inside, she knew she was dead. And as far as she was concerned, after not being able to contact Diamond or hearing anything from the lawyer, there was no chance of her ever seeing daylight. No dough, no chance! There was no way she was going to let the government take her life!

With that said, Ceazia packed up her belongings and placed them neatly in the corner. Then she removed the sheets from her bed. She stood with nothing but the flat sheet in her hand. She thought about all that she'd experienced throughout her life as she twisted the sheet tight, forming a makeshift noose. Ceazia didn't even bother saying a prayer as she positioned the noose perfectly and pulled a chair beneath it. She figured at this point not even God would save her. Hell was her destiny. Ceazia stood on the chair and placed the noose securely around her neck. "Fuck you! Fuck all of you! See ya in hell," were her final words before kicking the chair beneath her and hanging herself. She left no note or anything. On the real, who would really give a fuck?

It wasn't easy adjusting when Danielle got back to Atlanta. Of course, Richard got her a place of her own, but plenty of time was spent at his home. Pulling the typical baby mother moves. She called Richard and used her pregnancy as an excuse for attention. She knew when it came to Richard's child she could pull him in any direction she wanted. And since she'd heard the words "I love you" she was going to do all she could to see just how much. Danielle used every excuse in the book to be around Richard. "I'm feeling sick; the baby hasn't moved in a while; I'm weak; I'm in pain." Sure, Angel was still there for the time being, but when it came to Richard Anderson's child no one else mattered. And besides, Danielle Stevens always got what she wanted and her baby father was what she wanted. Now living comfortable, looking over the Buckhead area of Atlanta, she knew her time was coming. It wouldn't be long before she was back on top. She was at it again, rebuilding her fallen empire, but this time with a different approach.

With broken spirits but with California at her fingertips, Diamond was destroyed. It was because of her childhood that she'd always preferred women and only on the strength of Ceazia did she explore relations with men. When she was younger her foster father raped her repeatedly, but she never told anyone because she didn't want to be without a home. She vowed from then on that she would never let another man touch her body, but that all changed when she met Ceazia. She trusted and loved Ceazia so much that she would do anything to please her, including sacrificing her own happiness. Diamond relived a moment she'd hope to never experience again when Shawn raped her. Eager to put all memories behind her, she thought about her new life in California. There she would use the money from the little care package she sent herself to live out her dream and finally start a community dance school for girls. So, Ceazia wasn't the smartest fox after all. Diamond was one step ahead of everyone. She took twenty thousand dollars and sent it to California. She at least deserved that much; it wasn't easy playing her position because she too was a gangster's girl . . . Ceazia being that gangster!